I, Gloria Grahame

I, Gloria Grahame

Sky Gilbert

RARE
MACHINES

Publisher: Scott Fraser | Acquiring editor: Russell Smith
Cover design and illustration: Sophie Paas-Lang
Printer: Marquis Book Printing Inc.

Library and Archives Canada Cataloguing in Publication

Title: I, Gloria Grahame / Sky Gilbert.
Names: Gilbert, Sky, 1952- author.
Identifiers: Canadiana (print) 20200401696 | Canadiana (ebook) 20200401718 | ISBN 9781459748286 (softcover) | ISBN 9781459748293 (PDF) | ISBN 9781459748309 (EPUB)
Classification: LCC PS8563.I4743 I2 2021 | DDC C813/.54—dc23

We acknowledge the support of the Canada Council for the Arts and the Ontario Arts Council for our publishing program. We also acknowledge the financial support of the Government of Ontario, through the Ontario Book Publishing Tax Credit and Ontario Creates, and the Government of Canada.

Care has been taken to trace the ownership of copyright material used in this book. The author and the publisher welcome any information enabling them to rectify any references or credits in subsequent editions.

The publisher is not responsible for websites or their content unless they are owned by the publisher.

Printed and bound in Canada.

Rare Machines, an imprint of Dundurn Press
1382 Queen Street East
Toronto, Ontario, Canada M4L 1C9
dundurn.com, @dundurnpress 𝕐 f ⃝

to Ian, as ever

It was only briefly, as the door was open. I was doing my hair — I can't remember — on my way back from the bathroom, I think it was. And Nick was out. Honestly, I shouldn't have looked, I suppose, but then again there are some things that just stop you in your tracks. And why did I stop? It's fruitless to ask, really. No point at all. For I have no regrets. I, Gloria Grahame, do not, I repeat, do not regret.

"I was born when you kissed me. I died when you left me. I lived a few weeks while you loved me."

I wrote that line, or rather we wrote it together, though Nick and I don't do anything together anymore really, except, well, create. Anyway, I stopped. What of it? I looked in the doorway and the boy was lying on the bed naked, on his stomach, and the sheet was cast aside. Only slightly touching his right thigh. And I could see it all, it was all there, the adolescent — the glory of it all. He was just thirteen and I know that after glancing his direction I should have turned away. I did, in fact, turn away, but then I turned back and I couldn't help but notice the thick dark coat of adolescent fur on his legs, which I thought was precocious for such a young man, and reminded me — well, yes it did — of Nick. Not that Nick was on my mind. Only him. And the fact that he had, for that moment, supplanted Nick in my mind was enough to fill me; it filled me in that moment. And it was so nice to briefly be filled with something other than hate and rage.

So I turned back. And going beyond his leg to the curve of his buttocks, which were hairless and pink, and then pink, too, between his legs there was a hint of "it" — as his right leg was cocked, and for a moment I wanted to be the sheet that kissed his thigh. And then I turned away. It wasn't that I felt guilty, and why should I? Only that Nick would not like me looking, he never liked me looking — but not only at my stepson — looking was in itself a crime. And one thinks of how many times Nick — my dear husband for nearly two years (since 1948) and suddenly a "big" Hollywood director — has looked. And then there were the rumours. I've never told anyone this before — the rumours that Nick had some sort of "thing" for the actor Farley Granger. Have you heard that? I certainly heard it. He just loves Farley Granger, can't stop talking about him, and also seems very brave about talking about him, very unabashed, as if he has a right to just because he directed him in *They Live by Night*. But does that mean Nick owns Farley? Anyway, Nick always goes on about Farley Granger with this kind of bravado, praising him and even talking about how beautiful he was when he discovered him, and the fact of the matter is that nobody would ever have looked at that little homo if it wasn't for Nick.

And if you challenge him on it — well, I like to challenge him on it and see what happens. I like to see if he will hit me. Not that I want to be hit, no. I promise you I don't want to be hit. But it speaks to the power of Nick's mind and his body, which I'll have to admit is somewhat sexy. And I will goad him — Why not? It's fun — and say, "What went on between you and Farley Granger?" And he'll stop whatever he's doing and say, "You're not going to go there, are you?" And I'll say, "Maybe. Maybe I am going to go there," and then I'll ask him, "And exactly where would I be going?" looking him right in the eye. Once I even said to him, "Yes, I like to imagine you and Farley Granger in bed together." And he grabbed me, not unlike the way he is presently asking Humphrey Bogart to grab me in *In a Lonely Place*, and he shook me the way you shouldn't shake a baby, but I'm not a baby, I'm a woman who sometimes enjoys being shaken. And he was about to hit me. He almost hit me.

He has certainly hit me before, but frankly I don't re-member exactly when or how, as we were both drinking, and it was only that I woke up the next day and found the bruise. Once he kissed me on the bruise. I didn't like it, but there was something terribly tender about it because I know he was truly sorry. On the matter of whether or not I drive him into these rages — well, it's not at all a moot point. That is, of course I don't. Of course, it might appear that I do, to an onlooker (the only onlooker here, right now, is you, because yes, there is always someone looking, and that's not because I'm an egotist, it is, frankly, simply because I am a star). Well, the fact of the matter is that Nick rages. He rages constantly. I'm not sure at what, but there is always that rage.

The very first night I met him was at a bar in Hollywood, and I shouldn't have gone home with him that night, at least that is what mother says. (I take her direction about everything concerning the stage, but not in life.) At any rate, that night Nick was doing what he always does in bars, which is start fights. He was kidding some guy about his nose. It was a bulbous nose or a Cyrano de Bergerac nose; not a deformity, actually, but large. And Nick said something like "Do you find it gets in the way of things?" and this was enough to get the guy going with "What did you say? What did you say about my nose?" and Nick was loving it, I could see he was loving it, the fight, the thrill of the chase. "I was just wondering," he said, or something to that effect. And, of course, they ended up slugging it out until the bartender yelled at Nick, and I dragged him out of that bar. And this was our first date. An alarm should have gone off, I suppose. Well, it did. But what kind of alarm was it? It was an alarm saying this relationship *will not be boring.* Is this a good reason to get involved with anyone? No, in fact, perhaps the opposite. The law of attraction should be "I find this person very boring, ergo that person would be the perfect person to give me some peace and quiet, and ultimately put me to sleep." But we're a long-time dead, I say. Because I, Gloria Grahame, don't, when it comes down to it, give a you-know-what. For that very reason. And you might well consider that, too.

I, Gloria Grahame. It is certainly with a sense of some guilt that I write that. Or not guilt. Let's just say that it seems a kind of false freedom, because I am not. I can only be her for a short while, while pen is put to paper, or perhaps I should say more accurately, finger to keyboard — when I am writing whatever this is. (I don't call it anything, not even a diary or a journal, that would be too presumptuous.) She is certainly not me, and I have no relationship with her other than the fact that I do imagine I am this particular storied Hollywood film noir star, and I write as if I were her occasionally. But no one sees that writing. If you are reading this it is probably because I have been arrested finally or put to death. Good riddance, as they say. But all I do is fantasize that I'm Gloria Grahame. I am not her. I'm a very different person from her, and it's being completely honest to tell you that.

How do I begin to describe myself?

I have always been not very manly and somewhat invisible. Now that I am of a certain age, I wear hats and scarves, even in summer, and they serve to cover me somewhat, as I do not wish to be noticed. In fact, I wish to disappear; that is, short of dying. Why? It has basically become a little too much trouble to be alive. I think everyone reaches a point where that becomes the case and then they just die, one way or the other. That's my terribly depressing theory. It isn't that we outlive our usefulness or that nobody loves us, it's just that it finally isn't worth it anymore, the struggle. Anyway, first of all, or perhaps most of all, there is my voice. Have you ever heard Truman Capote's voice? You might google it, and if you do, you will discover that even for the most dedicated homophile it is just a little too much. I can't help it; I was born this way, to quote the great Gaga. When I open my mouth I betray myself. And yes, I always sashay a little bit, and there are mannerisms. But it is not a case of choosing to act this way; let me make that perfectly clear. If I had my way I would be someone else, I would be John Wayne, particularly the way he looked when he was young. (Did you know his real name was Marion?) Yes, I would prefer to be effortlessly masculine, which is the way I describe the type of man I am often attracted to. This makes me hopeless in a Quentin Crisp sort of way. I lust after the type of young man who would not be caught dead in public with me, which makes my case tragic, except of course for what you can get up to in private. But I pretty much don't bother with that anymore, either. So I have become this haunted thing, or rather this thing that would wish to be haunted or hunted, or something, but what I am really is just the type of person who makes people feel uncomfortable and who they would like more than anything to ignore.

Some women like me. *Some.* (Others, I threaten.) But it's more as if they take pity on me, and that is perfectly fine, too, it's something, anyway, it's someone actually having an emotion in regards to me, or perhaps I should say having an emotion in my direction or at least in my general vicinity. Which is certainly better than nothing. Or is it? When I was younger I made an effort to hide it, there were the scarves and hats back then, too — which, when you come down to it, accentuated it more than anything — if one adds sunglasses then one has become Greta Garbo, certainly not a very butch self-presentation. But there was also an attempt to monitor the voice and the hands and the hips, that is, to not be in any way myself, which I was sometimes successful at doing. Successful in the sense that people didn't so much *not* know that I was effeminate, but they quite generally appreciated the fact that I was doing my best to cover it up. It was gracious of them to notice, and gracious of me to try. I was being considerate of their sensibilities, trying not to offend.

And then in those days I did not have tenure. That's why I fought so hard for it, and now here I am teaching at a small university just outside of town. But I spend a lot of time in the city where I live. I spend a lot of time walking my dog, Poopsie. Yes, she is called Poopsie. Do what you want with that. The truth of the matter is that I would call her Poopsie, anyway, in private, so why not just make it public? It was bound to slip out, anyway. It's all part of giving up. My last dog was actually named Rex, which was comical in its own way because he was also a miniature poodle. I could carry him around in a canvas bag, which I would do now and then, and even take him to class. The problem was that he had cerebral palsy — yes, he did — and when I let him walk around the desk of the seminar room he would fall and quiver, and the students would think he was drunk. It was an interesting gauge of each student's moral compass. Some would laugh, the boys usually — the effortlessly masculine ones — whereas the girls would punch the boys' arms and be gushingly sympathetic to my little dog with CP. Anyway, calling this new little miniature poodle Poopsie is all part of giving up, the process of giving up who I am — while paradoxically being more publicly what I am. This is the beginning of a struggle not to exist anymore. Because though people might be able to tolerate a little poodle called Rex (there is, after all, humour in that) they are not about to care very much about one called Poopsie, and the male owner will be forever exiled from their consciousnesses. Out of sight, out of mind.

I hope you will applaud me in this end-of-life project; to fade from view long before I die. After all, it is quite evident that no one wants to see or hear from me anymore. In disappearing, I'm really just complying with the general zeitgeist. I'd ask for your advice — but you are, in fact, not there. I have just made you up in order to calm myself down. There must be someone reading this, even though it will never be read. And as I have imagined this, I also have imagined you, the same way I have imagined Gloria Grahame. You are somewhat sympathetic, but slightly frightened by me, and perhaps a bit confused? Because it seems to me that when I write as Gloria Grahame I am also able to write myself.

What does it mean to write yourself? It means what every writer knows: that they do not exist anywhere else but on paper, in the characters they create. That's true for me more so than anyone. Even T.S. Eliot — who was apparently nondescript and worked in a bank — was not as nondescript as me. Except for the afflictions that are my face, my body, my age, my fluttering hands. What happens to me is I come home after a hard day at school (it's two classes a day, twice a week — it must be admitted, I have absolutely nothing to complain about), and I am discouraged by the petty nothingness of my life, at how small even my humiliations are. And then I sit down and write this. I create. And everything that causes me discomfort, everything that causes me pain, is suddenly glorious. Glorious Gloria.

No, I cannot be her. Or can I? She is the opposite of what I am attracted to in a sexual way, she is effortlessly feminine and completely unashamed of everything that I am ashamed of. But she is not blithe; not unconscious of all the adoring male eyes turned on her, and the jealous female eyes politely turned away. But knowing the scandal stirred by her wake, she nevertheless carries on — something I battle daily to do.

My life, in fact, is crowded, not so much with incident as with tiny failures at being who I am expected to be as a male. Because she is female — and in touch with her feminine essence — Gloria is able to turn her much larger failures into triumphs.

I started writing as Gloria after a tiny child started hitting me in the leg at the bank. It didn't so much hurt as it was annoying, but I decided I wouldn't put up with it. So I leaned down to his general area nearer the floor, and said, "Please do not hit me, sir."

Well, when I stood back up again his mother was staring at me, furious. "Would you mind not talking to my son. Please keep away from my *family*." She used the word *family* — a kind of trigger for those like me who are perceived to be so grotesque or at least odd, so odd as to not deserve a loving family.

I stiffened, which doesn't look good on me, I'm sure. "But he was hitting me," I said.

"Please don't talk to my son," she said, turning him away from me as the child was, inevitably, fascinated by the spectacle.

And then she continued, "Don't talk to that man, don't talk to him, he's a bad man ... very bad ... you might ... get ... something." I shrank inside, all of me shrank, not just what you might imagine shrinking (*that's* usually pretty shrunken, anyway). Frankly, I wanted to die. I knew, of course, what she was referring to — AIDS. Well I went home immediately and wrote. I wrote like a fury, and invented Gloria.

You've probably never heard of Gloria Grahame, and you probably think you've never seen her in a movie. *But you have.* She played Violet Bick in *It's a Wonderful Life*. Remember? The town whore? Well, that's a bit of an overstatement. She was the as-close-to-a-whore as Hollywood would come in that wholesome movie — she was the sad and lonely "loose" girl in town, who flirts shamelessly with James Stewart. And then she played "the girl who can't say no" in the movie version of *Oklahoma*. That's what Gloria Grahame always played — she was born to play it — the bad girl. But more than that, the girl who couldn't help being bad, and on top of that, the girl who had a heart of gold. She was the epitome of femme fatale. And she was not perfectly beautiful (which she was very aware of) but instead just incredibly sexy. The most important thing about Gloria Grahame was that she could actually act. She came from an artistic family; her mother was an acting teacher, and her father was a writer. She knew what she was doing. And no matter how witless or promiscuous the girl she had been required to play, you just knew that she was centred, grounded, real, and owned her passion.

Well, the fantasy is that someday I will become her, that I will leave this body — the sad little effeminate man will disappear, and all that will be left will be the proud, lustful woman of my dreams.

I haven't mentioned the contract. The interesting thing about it is that Nick did not demand it himself and it is — to be perfectly accurate — not his fault. Bob Lord, the line producer, insisted on it, because he claims to have been in too many situations where husbands and wives work together and there is a tension that ruins the movie. Really, you must understand what it's like making a movie. There is a fake set constructed — a kind of box set for realism, or a backdrop if it's a cowboy movie — and you are in there, supposedly acting, while literally fifty to a hundred people — the technicians — surround you. Watching you. It's somewhat like acting in a play. There is an audience, because not only my acting in the scene but my behaviour, before and after the scene, are on display. As line producer, Bob must not only handle the budget for the film but also manage the day-to-day physical assets to the production. So he sits with the director, in one of those director chairs, watching everything. And what Bob is not aware of, and what is fully insulting to me, is that I am above all a consummate professional and, when it comes down to it, making a good movie is actually more important to me than any damn marriage.

I mean, I love/hate Nick, my husband — as any good wife does. Perhaps, in my case, it's less explicable. Nick is not particularly handsome — with his too-curly hair and too-large nose — so it is about something else. Animal magnetism? Thugishness? Extreme talent? I dare not say. But whatever my feelings about him on any particular shoot day, that doesn't mean I'd ever make a lousy movie because of them. I'm not entirely certain where I got this tendency, or if it is just a gene. It would be nice to say that I come from a theatrical family and I just picked it up through osmosis, but my sister is not at all like that; she couldn't care less if she made a good movie or a bad one, and, in fact, isn't interested in acting at all. And being a professional doesn't mean getting there on time or hitting your mark (although these things are important); it means giving the most honest performance possible, which means offering up a part of yourself, which is the very least any artist can do. It's probably sick or something that I need or want to do that — but audiences seem to like it. We'll see. So perhaps just because I am a "strong-willed woman," or perhaps because Nick is evidently nuts, the producer included this clause. I call it the "shut-up" clause.

I could actually call it the "no-nagging" clause because that is really the most outrageous part of it, and the part I resent most. Nagging is ours. We women own it, fully — and you can't take it away. It's really all we have. The men have the power. (Don't let anyone tell you that we rule men because we rule the bedroom. We do rule the bedroom, no doubt there, but it's horse do-do to suggest that because we rule the bedroom we rule anywhere else. We don't rule anything that matters and that's a fact.) Anyway, I'm proud to be a nag, because it's the only way I can actually have any effect in a man's world. So the fact that I am not allowed to "nag" my husband during the process of making this film is actually more galling to me than the primary clause — which says I'm not allowed to openly disagree with my husband. That I must *do as I am told.* I know that should gall me, but it doesn't. I've always been quite capable of pretending to do what I'm told and then going ahead and doing exactly the opposite. It's a secret that all actresses and most women employ to great effect.

But, anyway, it's not even so much the contract itself. What bothers me is that this is *supposedly* Bob Lord's edict, but it serves Nick's purpose, and ultimately, it serves Nick. The *company of men*; their damned brotherhood — it seems to operate automatically, without any acknowledgement on a conscious level. And I don't mean that it serves Nick that I have to do what I'm told. I can't stress too much that I rather like doing what I'm told and actually find it quite sexy. That's why the nag clause sticks in my craw. It's nagging that's really at the heart of it. It's our secret weapon; our only one. But no, it's that I am supposed to believe that Nick didn't initiate this, when it clearly was his wish and he is happier than hell to comply. And Nick actually, instead of telling me to shut up — or before telling me to shut up — actually calls up the damn clause and evokes Bob's name as if he was God or something. Jesus Christ, that burns me up. This is all Nick's idea, even if he won't admit it, or even if it wasn't his idea — because he's such a damned charming egotist, which is why I love him. But you can't even get a word in edgewise sometimes. I mean, I wouldn't want a man who would let me get a word in edgewise — but then when it happens I want to kill him. I'll tell you what it is — it's that he is ultimately threatened because it is a woman who disagrees with him and a woman who is right. Sure, Nick wants never to be wrong with anybody, but there's something he gets out of shutting *me* up particularly. *That* burns my ass, let me tell you. No, it's more than that. Tony — his first son by his previous marriage — actually made me realize it.

You know, Nick didn't always used to be like this. Tony is a remarkably perceptive young man, and he clocked the moment when Nick started to act this way. He said that when he was a kid — a little kid — Nick was just, well, fun — or at least that's the way Tony remembers him. And then, when Tony was about nine years old, Nick turned into a "Dad." In the most stereotypical way.

I wonder if this happens to all men. I don't think it had anything to do with Tony or actually being a father. I think it had to do with power. When they started allowing Nick to direct feature films, when he began to get a little public recognition for what he really wanted to do, he began to turn into a, well, a patriarch. It's all this avuncular-ness, it just makes me want to slap him; it's not even sexy, like his rage, it's just incredibly annoying. There's something he does where he just seems to think he knows more than you do. He does it to Tony, he does it to me, and, true, Tony is a child and I am a woman, but does that excuse it? Isn't he taking advantage? What about "all creatures great and small?" I mean, really? What about our rights? Even as the secondary human beings we are — what about them? So what do I do? I'll tell you what I'll do. I'll nag the hell out of Mr. Nicholas Ray, because I know it drives him crazy, and if he starts yelling about the contract I'll just tell him to go away because he can't take away a woman's God-given right to nag. I hate to be so graphic but it's kind of like cutting off my tits. Tits and nagging. Hey, take my word for it, we need them. I mean, would you send a soldier out to war with an unloaded gun?

* * * * * *

It feels so good to write this, disappearing into the study of my apartment. I must describe my apartment to you. It's a cozy nook I happened to find by chance. There is a wonderful bay window at the front that looks out onto the city street and there are trees, believe it or not, and then a small galley kitchen and a bathroom (the less said the better) and then at the back the coziest nook — my study — or what I call my study, for I sleep in the living room on a pullout couch. But here, at the very back of the apartment, with my little gabled window, I write. I am safe here from all attack and can imagine Gloria in all her glory.

I must say that this disappearing thing is not such a new thing for me. It is and it isn't. That is, I have always disappeared, but actually not to this extent. It has always been easy to ignore me, and often I am treated as someone with a disability. The most sympathetic woman in the room is the one who inevitably turns to me, and perhaps even calls me "dear." I am regularly called "dear" by waitresses. I'm sure they call other people dear — but, I fear, perhaps not as regularly as me. There is a general tone of condescension when it comes to me, because I am quite obviously too homosexual for words. There is probably no way to really describe how effeminate I am.

When I tell people that I am a tenured professor — and it is just sometimes necessary to do that, for practical reasons, not bragging — they inevitably say, "Good for you!"

Good for you. Really, honestly, can you believe that? But what is beyond the pale is that they have no idea how condescending they are being; they honestly believe that I should take it as a compliment. So, outside of this kind of marginalization, I am basically ignored already. It's just that there was a time when I wasn't quite so prepared to surrender myself to such ignominy. This had a lot to do with the fact that there were certain persons who once found me sexually attractive — this was long, long ago, when I was young. There was a brief period when I could fool people into thinking I was attractive, but even when I hit thirty it was beginning to go. When I hit thirty-five it was completely gone. I do have a very slender build, still to this day, but I have developed somewhat of a paunch. And I say "somewhat" accurately. It is a small paunch, relatively speaking, and I can see how I might still be perceived as slender. Or at least, slight. But there was a time when I would walk into a room, and it wasn't so much that all eyes would turn to me, as it would be that — quite often, in a large room, filled with many people — one pair of eyes would turn in my direction, and I could see desire in those eyes. Desire for the slender, weak torso, the limp white arms, and, of course, the slight roundness of my buttocks (always a plus). I did not exactly have a pretty face, but I was boyish looking for a time (though my mouth is small and mealy). It all fed into a certain kind of fantasy, and the men who wanted me would be large, some very large, and they were each to protect me and have their way with me.

I only wish that more of them had actually been flush with cash. I don't know how I avoided it — that is, getting a rich husband. I guess I don't have the knack for it (unlike Gloria, whose third husband was Cy Howard, a hugely successful comedy writer and television producer — think *The Smothers Brothers*), which is why I went back to school and decided to teach. For a while there were some theatrical aspirations, but when I lost my looks — meaning my good looks *and* the men stopped looking — I knew it was time to acquire a trade. I have one friend who is physically equipped much like myself — he is small and thin and has a very affected, girlish voice, but he is constitutionally incapable of sleeping with anyone except older men who are very rich, who own at least one house. He has approximately three houses now (I say approximately because one was in escrow) all from the estates of his elderly exes who have all died. This was very practical of him; I am not equipped with his practicality.

But I was speaking of disappearing, and how at one time I was still somewhat visible, only because some men wanted occasionally to sleep with me. You see, I am not capable of actually wooing someone, of initiating anything, of taking an active role in any way whatsoever. I wait for them to come to me; and sure enough my vulnerability and quiet shy manner attracts, or used to attract, eventually, someone. But even then — and this is the essence of it — even then, when attention was paid to me, I understood this as a sort of aberration, as a colossal mistake really, an accident that happened to have a fruitful outcome. I was ashamed of people being attracted to me, because it just seemed to me so perverse. I mean, why would they be? But if I was attracted to them, I would let them have their way with me. And now, well, it just — I know how grotesque I must appear to the young. I can't imagine that they would ever find me attractive. Hence the hats and scarves and Poopsie.

But there are moments when I — and this is what I am writing about really — moments when I still harbour the odd hope. I really don't wish to call it hope because that makes it seem positive when I think it is probably demented. So I harbour a demented hope, and this is something I think I should stamp out of my measly little soul. What shape does this demented hope take? Occasionally, there are moments when someone seems to be attracted to me, and I am very sorry for them, unsure exactly what it might all be about, but it seems somehow to be related to the fact that I was once their teacher. There, I said it. And there is *Venus and Adonis*, another demented hope, but I dare not talk about that.

I'm sitting at home today, as I'm not required on set, sipping a coffee in the kitchen at 567 Crestline Drive in Brentwood, feeling cozy under our lovely Spanish-style red roof. This house was very unwelcoming when I moved in. Nick had no taste at all — or what he had was spare. It was my job to cozy it up, and at the moment I am looking at the boldly red flowered curtains — the pattern of which Nick has appropriated for our film *In a Lonely Place*. This I find mildly unsettling.

What am I thinking? Well, I happen to be thinking about one of the things that has been a source of inspiration for me lately — that I am such a good mother. I'm not praising myself; it came as somewhat of a surprise. During my pregnancy I must admit that I was intimidated by the whole thing, but it was the height of my love for Nick. He adored me, it seems, pretty unceasingly, or unceasingly enough. Shall I tell you the way Nick "does it"? I don't want to say that foul word so I'll just say that he makes love to me in a kind of a frenzy. He's usually drunk. And there is something about it that suggests he wishes it to be over. It is, in a word, hurried — there is no foreplay, he just gets right down to it — which is fine with me; I can't tell you how many times I've had to endure the fumbling, irritating caresses of a man who is trying to give me what I want. To hell with what I want, just get on with it, and either you'll be what I want or not. Nick is not well-endowed, particularly, but he is substantial, and the way he goes at it is with a kind of fierce dedication. He somewhat attacks me and holds me down and has his way with me, and then he pummels me, sexually. That's the only word for it. It's a bit angry, and it's as if he is trying desperately to release himself in me.

I know for some women this might seem like a nightmare, or at least far too similar to rape, but honestly, with me that's not an issue. Quite the contrary. But there is an element of it that makes it seem that he is glad when it is over, as if he just wants to get it all out of the way. It is desire, and it is intense, and I help him get rid of it. When it's over he will often get up, immediately, and have a cigarette. He will hand me one, of course (he's not a beast).

I don't know how I got onto that all of a sudden. Oh, yes, he continued to pummel me, sexually, throughout the pregnancy; I had to assure him that he would not hurt the baby (men have such an inflated sense of themselves). And so I was quite happy to be pregnant, and I didn't go through that thing that so many women do of feeling unattractive. Of course, I had to hide the pregnancy behind car doors and whatever, because Hollywood thought that it was impolite for a star to be pregnant, or that it was not proper for a sex symbol (although I certainly don't wish to see myself that way, it's part of my job, like any other). And then when I had the baby it was relatively painless — now, with the drugs, you hardly know you're having one — but suddenly I was ecstatic and all that mother juice, or whatever it is, began to flow into my veins. I wanted to protect Timmy and love him, and all my energy went into the nursery and taking him to the doctor and just generally being concerned.

He was somewhat frail at first, but then all babies are — or seem to be.

But then what became irksome was that it seemed to me that Nick was suddenly suspicious. Where did that come from? He didn't seem to trust me, trust that I could actually *be* mothering, and then when I actually became a mother and did fully what was expected of me (perhaps even more) he would shoot me these ironic looks. I would tell him that I'd be right downstairs because I had to burp the baby — and I really did love burping him.

There was a mirror in the nursery, and I know it sounds bizarre, but I would look at myself with the baby there, by my shoulder, looking all content as I was burping him, and I was so enchanted by the picture. And Nick actually came up to the nursery and he stood there staring at me with Timmy and it was very odd. I asked, "What are you looking at?"

He said, "Nothing." He just smiled and shook his head. And then he continued looking at me.

I said, "Why don't you take a picture? It lasts longer." And he shook his head and smiled and then just continued looking. And I said again, "Really, what *are* you looking at?"

"I just don't believe it," he said. And that really galled me.

I thought, *What are you saying? Are you saying you don't believe I'm actually burping the baby? Well, I am.* But I didn't say that; I just said, "Go and eat your dinner. I'll be there momentarily," and he finally left our cavernous nursery — the largest bedroom located at the rear of our ranch-style house. Shaking his head, chuckling to himself.

Really, the balls of that guy. Honestly, I don't mean to be vulgar, but how dare he suggest that it is odd for me to be a mother? It really does make me quite angry. I don't see the contradiction in being a sultry sex siren or whatever else I'm supposed to be. I just don't see what's so damn paradoxical about a woman like me being a mother. It's completely insulting. I am a mother, it's instinctual, inside me, and I have a baby, and I'm one of the best mothers you'll ever see. And if Nick has some hare-brained idea that I am going to get tired of it, then he's got quite a surprise coming. I can and will continue to be as sensitive and have as many *feelings* as any other woman. Why do you think the whore with a heart of gold is such a cherished stereotype? Because all women, all real women, know that you are required to be both. And if you are any sort of woman at all, you will be. And I am a *real* woman of course. No matter how much artifice goes into my cinematic creations.

As Gloria goes on about her "realness" I feel, writing this, that perhaps she doth protest too much, and thus I feel a necessity to speak about my situation. It's not pretty, meaning that I am at a point in my life when I should be disappearing, I have settled on disappearing, but there is suddenly this last gasp of, well, of being alive, or trying to live, through my art — or what I imagine to be my art.

In my dotage, you see, I have been teaching Shakespeare. It took me a lot of self-convincing to start teaching it; my specialty used to be nineteenth-century British playwrights. I always wanted to teach Shakespeare, but I didn't have the courage. I think you might know what I mean, it just seemed so daunting, and very male, or masculine, or at least somewhat incomprehensible — how was one ever to dare to call oneself an expert? It's almost written in a foreign language. And how was I to own all that authority? I'm not Harold Bloom. Then I began to read various theories about Shakespeare either being gay or being a woman. I, for one, prefer the Queen Elizabeth theory.

At any rate, I began to tell myself that Shakespeare was not male in the way that I had always imagined him, and then I re-read *Twelfth Night* and I tried to find a single male character in it who was a "real man" in any conceivable sense of the phrase. And I couldn't find one. I mean Orsino is a lazy poetic fop who lolls about on divans and prates about love and falls in love with a girl who he thinks is a boy. Andrew Aguecheek is a skinny flaxen-haired dimwit drunk who imagines himself brave and is not, and Sir Toby is a fat dimwit drunk of the same ilk. Antonio appears to be in love with Sebastian — Sebastian who has his mother's ways and looks exactly like his sister. And, finally, there is Malvolio. I can't help identifying with him. I am often the one who spoils the party — you know, insists that they turn the music down. I don't know why that is. Next to my lovely downtown flat that I have had for many years, there are always, for some reason, new neighbours, and I am always standing out in the hallway knocking on their door. I do expect them to at some point say to me — as Andrew does to Malvolio — "Dost thou think, / because thou art virtuous, / there shall be no more cakes and ale?"

Not that I am virtuous — far from it — but I know because of my mannerisms and my age, people will insist on seeing me as a prissy, Malvolio-esque fellow. I know my students do. It actually makes me feel quite safe that they other me in such a way; the distance is reassuring. I am forgiven my eccentricities because professors are supposed to be that way. To the students we are strange and demented creatures who do something most of them find trying in this day and age. That is, we read. So now that I have examined Shakespeare's plays and found endless evidence of a kind of alternative attitude to sex and sexuality, it only makes sense to me that I might teach his works.

Perhaps Queen Elizabeth wrote the plays in secret and that's why the men are so often weak or evil — and if they are strong, as in Coriolanus or Antony, Macbeth or Lear, they find themselves naked on a heath, or divesting themselves of their armour, being emasculated by their wives, or admiring the beauty of a male enemy.

It was probably *Richard II* that really confirmed my idea that Shakespeare must have been either woman or a man such as I am, a kind of half man — a bend-over-and-pick-up-the-soap sort of fellow.

Richard II is such an old queen, he really is, and he calls himself "nothing" over and over, which has lately been my mantra. All the more appropriate because the Elizabethan slang word for a woman's genitalia was "nothing" (i.e., *Much Ado About Nothing*) so when he goes on and on about being "nothing" he is, in actuality, calling himself a vagina.

But the breakthrough work for me was *Venus and Adonis*, which is not a play but a poem, and I want to change all that.

It is a vain dream, a dream in vain, but I continue to nurture it, though I am sure to be struck down soon, because I am, like Richard II, nothing (no quotation marks, please). Perhaps I even have this insane idea of turning *Venus and Adonis* into a play because I want it to fail, and it is all a kind of aesthetic or theatrical masochism. For though the possibility of making a play out of the classic poem seems to shrink every day, I still return to it — which ultimately just guarantees what is sure to be relentless future humiliation. I was inspired to love this poem because no one else does, and its neglect is quite upsetting.

Venus and Adonis concerns an older woman's unabashed lust for a teenage boy. When Venus (the goddess of love) sees the beautiful young Adonis, she falls in love with him. He's a dedicated sportsman — a hunter — and not interested in women. She tries to persuade him with kisses and rhetoric. While on the hunt, Adonis is gored by a wild boar. Well, we know what that's all about. It's a wound on his thigh, but it's quite apparent to anyone with a metaphorical eye that since Venus doesn't have the appendage to actually fuck him, he has been allegorically fucked up the bum by a pig. Mourning for him, she decrees love will always be painful and contradictory. The subject matter is largely verboten; most critics are not able to deal with Venus's unabashedly pornographic intergenerational desire, calling her selfish or appalling. Of course she is both those things, and that's what makes her wonderful.

Although the poem is somewhat impossible for many scholars to get their heads around, I teach it — and the students are quite thrilled. I must mention the end where Venus curses love: "Sorrow on love hereafter shall attend: / It shall be waited on with jealousy, / Find sweet beginning, but unsavoury end." This prophetic conclusion makes the poem's complex verbiage worthwhile. *Venus and Adonis* is an early modern jewel of cynical paradox: "Sith in his prime Death doth my love destroy, / They that love best their loves shall not enjoy."

Now "true love" is — as far as I know — impossible. I've only experienced it in (what can I say?) the most embarrassing and hopeless ways. But even those who are actually in love with a real person — and struggling with the contradictory emotions that entails — will find Venus's curse deeply moving. The youngsters who are in my classes and all love-struck or sex struck — or whatever they are — just seem to adore thinking and writing about this poem.

But my idea, and I am almost ashamed to say this, is to bring a new theatrical invention to the world that will completely "queer" *Venus and Adonis*. Adonis will be played by a beautiful boy, but also — and this, I like to imagine, is truly innovative — even Venus herself will be played by a beautiful boy.

There will be no casting couch; I am not capable of such atrocities, but it would nevertheless be an adventure to put the whole thing together. The problem is that I have submitted this idea, my magnum opus, to the city's arts council, and I am waiting with bated breath to be rejected. I am sure that I will be rejected, and the failure of the project will just be fodder for my eventual disappearance and ultimately, my death.

"Old Man, Unable to Get Play Produced, Drinks Arsenic."

But that is too dramatic. No one cares about this old man. He simply disappears one day; no one is sure how, and no one cares why.

We're in the trailer, which is located just outside the stage door. The door to the trailer is open (as is the rather large stage door), because if it was closed we might be suspected of arguing or — something else. The trailer is well appointed of course — the stars are always taken care of. In his maniacal fashion, Nick has recovered the trailer's kitchen seats and the only chair with the red flowered material identical to the curtains in our kitchen at home; he has also used the same material to decorate the set. This is somewhat unhinged of him. He couldn't bother to decorate his own house until I got there, but now he is meticulous about every detail of the film set *and* of my trailer.

Well, right now we're having an argument about lipstick. I shouldn't allow it. I should have put my foot down, but there's the contract again, nipping at my heels. I'm not supposed to argue, so I tell Nick I'm not arguing; we're just having a discussion. I don't raise my voice; wouldn't want Bob Lord or anyone else to hear raised voices in the trailer and then peek in. Though we are arguing, I sill smile and flirt with him, which always helps, and do that thing I do, which is to lower my head and look up at him from below my eyelashes. And then, of course, I add "the pout," which is icing on the cake, but nevertheless *de rigueur.*

Most women who know their stuff are aware of this technique; it's timeworn but utterly efficient. The lowered-head-while-looking-up-at-him position is a gentle nod to fellatio, a kind of reference to it, any time that your head is even slightly lowered and you are looking up at a man you are making reference to that sexual act and any woman worth her salt knows it. I am eternally attracted to Nick, always have been, always will be, it's his authority and passion that excite me, and so I can't stop myself from flirting with him, even when I hate his guts.

I have discovered a way of applying lipstick that is truly revolutionary. I think that I may have invented it; although I must have seen it somewhere. I'm sure I have, I just can't remember where. I do hope it wasn't on a whore. But then again, who cares? The technique is this: you apply, in a best-case scenario, three colours of lipstick. The colours, of course, have to be closely related, not just different shades of red, but very slightly varied shades of sister colours — you wouldn't want, for instance, to be applying an orange-red and a pink-red lipstick together in a "*ménage.*" You would either want to proceed with three slightly different orange-red shades or three slightly different pink-red shades. There are three areas of the lips: there is the outer area, beyond your actual lips — I always paint a little above and below my own lips because they are simply not quite big enough — there is the lip itself, and, finally, there is the middle or inside of the lip, which is where you add the third colour. You must be subtle, beyond just the shades that you pick, you must blend, deftly. If you have applied it correctly then people will be quite startled, and in the best-case scenario they will be very attracted to you but they won't know exactly why.

Well, Nick would have none of it. As soon as I appeared on set he walked over to me and gently placed his hand on my arm. At least he didn't dress me down in front of Bogie. That is always the threat. Nick's been known to dress me down in public before. I have enormous respect for Humphrey Bogart, who — even though he is a somewhat instinctive actor — is always spot on and breathlessly charming (he plays the tortured leading character of *In a Lonely Place*). So Nick spared me that humiliation but released a vicious, hissing whisper, "What are you doing?"

I asked him what he meant by that question. "Your lipstick?" I acted dumb, which has worked more often that you might think. "We need to go back to your trailer."

"But ..."

"What?"

"Do you want a scene here? Now?

"No. But ..."

"Now." I turned and strode back to the trailer, but not without smiling at Bob Lord and waving. It worked like a charm. Bob didn't suspect anything.

When we got in the trailer I asked, "What do you mean 'my lipstick'?"

"I mean, what's going on with all the colours?"

"It's just three colours. And don't be so melodramatic."

"You have to wipe it off."

"Don't be ridiculous. I'm not going to wipe off my lipstick."

"We're in the trailer now. You can put on one colour."

"No."

"Are you arguing with me?'"

"Yes," I said.

"Well, Bob is here. He's watching us. If we stay in here too long he'll come in here looking for us. So we have to sort this out."

"Well if he does I'll just smile at him and make it right. Why are you asking me to do this? I at least have a right to ask why."

"Because you look like a ..." he stared at me. "You know what you look like."

"No, I don't. Tell me," I said, staring him down. I wanted to hear him say it.

"A whore," he said, quite satisfyingly. It was worth the whole episode just to hear him almost call me a whore. It revved me up like crazy and I knew it was doing the same for him. And then he added, quite scornfully, "How many times do I have to tell you that you're playing a nice woman? Or is that beyond your comprehension?"

I walked into the bathroom and shut the door, but in a very relaxed manner so it wouldn't rock the trailer.

What I savour in these moments is that Nick has no idea what I'm up to when it comes to my face. My face has never been entirely satisfactory, at least not to me, and if Nick knew what I did to it, he would be furious. But it's none of his business because it's my face.

My face, you see, has never been quite right. It seems right to other people, but they don't really know, or they don't see it as I do, which is through the eyes of perfectionist. And there are things I can have done, there are treatments that are not invasive, which are performed by a licensed doctor. Basically, it's all about making my upper lip somewhat firm and larger. The doctor occasionally gives me this little help. The only problem is that for the time that he is doing the treatments I can't have Nick kiss me. This is irksome. I claim headaches, am generally ill. I honestly do not like this time when I can't make myself available to his wishes, and I know it frustrates the hell out of him. For a while it can be fun to tease him, but then he gets very frustrated and even threatening. I always manage to put him off. I don't dare tell him. He would be very angry at me and accuse me of being insecure; but a woman, for obvious reasons, has to be. It's a lot of work, you know, being beautiful, and it's completely likely that it all might just suddenly disappear.

* * * * * *

I must tell you something else that I am quite ashamed of. It's the way I keep things under control at school. What do I have to keep under control? Well, what you might think; my desires for my male students. I must begin by stating explicitly that there has never been any sort of impropriety whatsoever and there never will be. I am appalled by professors who sleep with their students. It isn't so much a moral problem as a practical one. By that I mean that it simply cannot be compatible with effective teaching. How could you concentrate on the matter at hand? On pedagogy? It's one thing to desire them, we all desire them, and any teacher who claims not to is just lying, or not human.

But I am a teacher, you see, who relies on my charm. I know that it takes quite a while for me to charm the students, as they are slightly alarmed by me at first, because even when my effeminacy is under control, it's threatening to some. But once they have gotten used to me (one can get used to anything; it's a terrifying human trait!) I am able to make them laugh, usually through self-deprecation in reference to my advanced age, which they, of course, relish. So from the start I am setting up a situation of disadvantage, and I work like a beast to make it more so. In other words, if any young men in my class appear in any way to be attracted (I know, unlikely), I do everything in my power to make them unattracted to me, short of gaining weight or deliberately maiming myself. But I do maim myself metaphorically, to coin a phrase. I present myself as an antique squirrelly freak of nature wrapped up in his ancient books and classical music (which is all too true) who barely sees the light of day (my skin is a sort of unsensuous porcelain, if you can imagine, and unalluringly translucent, except when I use a tanning machine, which is rare), and my lips are, by nature, alarmingly thin. I am glad of all this because it is necessary to teach. It is necessary for me to be a kind of quirky entertaining being from another place and time. Thus, none would ever approach me, my office hours are mostly empty, young men are particularly terrified of me, and that's fine, because I could not ever be involved with them in that way and teach them.

Oh yes, there are those who go on about pedagogy as sexual, but I am not one of them. We are not Greeks. I could not teach if I allowed myself to act on desires that I will not deny are there. Because no teacher can actually teach if those very private feelings are actually acted upon. And it is an abuse of power to do such a thing. They look up to you, like stray puppies, even when you are not worth looking up to, and it is a crime to betray that trust. I understand all that completely — but when that relationship is over and they've had time away from school, I think to myself, *Might it happen, ever, naturally?*

That is not to say that I wouldn't, in this context, have every right to stray from the beaten path. Oh dear me, when I went to university so many years back I took one or two electives that were theatre courses. I took movement and even tumbling — I was actually quite limber back then. Anyway, the teacher of movement was a statuesque man of colour whom I respected enormously. He was very silent (being a movement teacher, this was somewhat to be expected), so I imagined him to be a noble person. I've always been intimidated by silent people; I assume that they are judging me when this may very well be the furthest thing from their mind. I feared and respected him; he just seemed to exude integrity. So I *thought*. Well, years later, after I graduated I encountered a woman who had been in the same movement class. She held a contract teaching position where I was teaching at the time. We started talking about this man, and I praised him for what I perceived to be his integrity.

She laughed and said, "He was trying to get into everyone's pants."

"Everyone's?" I asked.

She said, "Well, strictly speaking, just the girls'." She went on and on about how he imagined himself a proper Lothario and indeed was one and had slept with many of my fellow female students. She said that she had to beat him off with a stick. This was extremely shocking. I put it down to my homosexuality that I was simply not conscious of any of the straight sexual intrigues bubbling around me. And, further to this point, several professors where I teach (elderly males) are married now to young women who were once their teaching assistants — and before that, their graduate students. And several of my colleagues are married to other professors in the unit. However you look at it, it is a veritable cesspool of heterosexuality that goes on behind closed doors in our English department, and a good proportion of it is age inappropriate.

I certainly don't think this activity gives me any right to proposition my male students; on the other hand, I don't feel ashamed of my feelings, nor the fact that I have negotiated a plan for circumventing disaster.

When I first began at this institution, I went out to lunch with an elderly homosexual professor. It was suggested that I do so by of one of my colleagues. "You will love him," she said. "You will have so much in common." He is dead now, so I can tell you his name: David Eagle. Professor Eagle was a world-renowned expert on Marlowe. Marlowe is boring; I can't bear to read him. But my female friend didn't know that, or perhaps she was referring to my Elizabethan scholarly interests, somehow — however, those inclinations were only nascent then. Thus my suspicion/fear is that she imagined our compatibility would be based on something *much more sinister*.

After a couple of lunches with Professor Eagle it became utterly and shockingly clear that his primary occupation in life was obsessing about young male students. He went on and on about falling in love with them; it was not entirely clear whether or not he had actually had sex with them, though it seemed eminently possible, and it seemed to happen while they were his students during the school year, which I found appalling. Most of his talk was concerned with tortured luncheons and coffees with these beautiful young men and the inkling to put his hand on their thighs, or how he used to gaze at them over a restaurant table. The boys would put him off, and then he hoped they would eventually give in, et cetera. Yuch. A completely betrayal of pedagogical standards, and a plague on those poor students who depended on him for knowledge and marks (!) having to put up with his inappropriate advances.

I tried to indicate my discomfort with these talks, but he didn't get the message. I had to stop meeting him because, as I was considerably younger than he, it also occurred to me that he might at some point become obsessed with me, and there was absolutely nothing I found attractive about him. I've tried to pretend that I have nothing in common with Professor Eagle but I'm not certain that, in one sense at least, it is perfectly true, though the hopelessness of his obsessions — and their explosiveness — impressed me heavily.

Since ending my friendship with him (was he the cause of what was to follow? No, the seeds were there ...) several young men in my classes have caught my eye. I have always studiously avoided any personal chats with them, and if they do find it necessary to make an appointment with me in my office, I keep the door open during our talk. I have had to make some compromises because there have been certain students who were simply too beautiful for words, and it was difficult for me even to look at them. The compromise was only in the form of a promise to myself.

I must admit that I find it difficult to imagine a world in which there would not be a fraction of a chance that I might someday permit myself to fall in love with, well, perhaps one of my *ex*-students? That is, hopefully very long after they were my student? When there would no longer be the power dynamic people so often speak of that makes such a flirtation so clearly wrong? The thought that I might not be able to ever fall in love with one of my students — at any point in my life *après* teaching — just makes life unbearable, as there are no prospects for anything in my life of a romantic nature, and the very praxis of the classroom experience is sometimes exciting in a certain way. I imagine that somehow, out of this bond, a pedagogical intimacy may arise, so to speak. If I were to feel this kind of connection with one of my students in the class — perhaps over a discussion of *Venus and Adonis*, for instance — I would mentally clock them in, put their face and heavenly body in my memory bin, and hold them there, with the promise to myself that one day, when the student graduated, if I happened to see them at a gay bar, or even in a public place, and if I found that they were not repelled by my presence, that I might … respond. As I am not actually capable of pursuing anyone, this would take the form of them pursuing me. And if this happened, as long as the time period that elapsed was over two years (I am very strict about this, in my own mind), and as long as I could see no possibility of said younger person ever becoming a graduate student *anywhere* (you never know when a stray graduate student will turn up!), well, if that student wanted to pursue me I would not say no. In fact, I would say an enthusiastic yes — and my romantic fantasies might come to fruition.

I keep this at the back of my mind and it is one of the things that allows me to continue teaching, because it isn't only that I love Shakespeare's work, it's that there is still the faintest possibility that someday — at the end of the comedy, at the conclusion of the tragedy — there will be, well, a young man.

It's only started recently but now I am convinced that *In a Lonely Place* — a film about a man suspected of committing a murder (and the woman who loves him) — is a film about my husband. What I mean is, what started out as a faithful adaptation of a novel has become the story of Mr. Nicholas Ray, and I'm not certain I'm entirely comfortable with it. Not that I have a choice. Never mind the no-nagging clause, it does appear that I am trapped somewhat in a web of Nick's own devising. It's all too Hitchcockian for words — perhaps Nick has Hitchcock on his mind. It's more than unsettling that the novel is about a murderer, but since I know for a fact that Nick is not a murderer (I suppose that's not an absolute certainty — I mean, what is? — but it's certainly highly unlikely, or at least unlikely *enough* that he is one) then the film could not be about him because he's not a murderer. Because I'm not so much saying he might be murderer … but actually, yes, that *is* what I'm saying. And this is the revelation, now that I think of it. If *In a Lonely Place* is not about a confirmed murderer anymore — now it has become a film about a man who *might possibly be* a murderer — this makes the movie much more sinister.

A movie about a murderer is a whodunit, and when it's over we all know who the murderer is, and we feel a lot safer. But a movie about an ordinary man — any ordinary man— like Nick, who might be a murderer, is much more disturbing, because suddenly you start to look at the man beside you in a different way. And that's what's happened to me: I can't help wondering if this is that what Nick wants. Does Nick want me to think he's a murderer? Or at least a threat? Is that what making this movie is really all about? Trying to make me afraid of him? I must say all of this manipulation makes me very angry and suspicious. Because lately the dynamic has become complex. He owes so much money that he literally gave me trouble the other day over buying a dress. I said to him, "Nick, this has to stop." And he said, "What has to stop?" And I said, "If a girl can't even buy a dress there is something terribly wrong. How much do you actually owe?" And he said it was none of my business. And I said that as his wife, it certainly was.

This led to a very nasty fight, which didn't get physical, at least in a nasty way, though we did end up making up, which was fun enough.

Honestly, sometimes I think it's time to put sugar in his pills again. Nick takes these pills, and I'm not sure exactly what they are but I know they contribute to his gambling addiction — and it is an addiction — and I know that he always takes them before he goes out in the evening. My mother and I — I'm almost ashamed to say it, but it was her idea — one night we filled all his pills — which are in capsule form —

with sugar. He went out that night (when doesn't he?) and I saw him take the pills, and he didn't seem to notice. I mean sugar does hop you up, doesn't it? But not in the way that amphetamines do.

We were out last night at a party for Maxwell Shane's new film *City Across the River*, a film about a juvenile delinquent, which wasn't very good. Well, it was good for what it was, I guess — a truly B picture. But Nick liked the adaptation and was thinking of working with Maxwell on some novel he's got ahold of, which is also about a juvenile delinquent. Anyway, Nick's high on his pills that certainly aren't filled with sugar and there's this divine young man walking around. The agent Arnold Buttson (Nick calls him Arnold Buttkiss!) just discovered him selling apples in the audience in an off-Broadway production of *The Threepenny Opera*. Well the boy has potential, no doubt about that. At the moment he has a very nasal Bronx accent. His name is Anthony Curtis but the studio is thinking of changing his name. There's something about him, I would like to say a star quality, and it might be that, but it's really just an alluring mischievousness, very streetwise, very working class — and those eyes? Really, it's difficult to stop looking at him. And it's quite clear he would sleep with anybody. He may even have slept with Arnold Buttkiss. (An agonizing thought!) So we were lolling about at the party and I was trying not to look at Anthony Curtis *too* much and then — out of the corner of my eye — I caught Nick staring at him. I couldn't believe it, or rather I could believe it, but it appalled me. First Farley Granger, now Anthony Curtis? That made me want to talk to this young whippersnapper. So I left Nick, who was just so drunk and hopped-up, anyway — and so wanting to talk to the director who was our host, Maxwell Shane — that he didn't even notice.

I went right up to this very appealing young man and chatted. He was shameless. He has these extra-long lashes and he actually did the "fellatio look" at me! Yes, he lowered his head and looked up at me from underneath his eyebrows. And I thought, *What is he hinting at?* The female equivalent of you-know-what? I'm certainly not averse to such an activity; Nick rarely gets up to it — or *down to it*, I suppose I should say — and when he does he's usually so drunk that he can't remember where anything is, and ends up paying attention to me *in that general area*, which is more frustrating than actually erotic. So here I was trying to lure young Anthony into propositioning me, not that I would have done anything — my bark is worse than my bite — and Nick suddenly appears beside me and grabs me hard by the arm — there will be a bruise — and wrenches me away with nary an "excuse me" to Anthony! He dragged me into a dark corner in another room (Shane may be only a B-movie director but he has one of the biggest houses in Hollywood, go figure. He has giant ferns everywhere, perilously high ceilings, and even stone lions — indoors. Does he think this will all get him a job at Metro-Goldwyn-Mayer?) and started hissing at me, "What do you think you're doing?"

I told him that I was flirting with a very beautiful young man with very beautiful young eyelashes, and he threw down his drink (it made a mess), grabbed my shoulders, shook me in that way he has been lately, and said, "What gives you the right to do that?"

And I told him that though I was married and had a child that didn't mean I had given up flirting. "I'm not going to *do* anything with him," I said.

"Oh, I guess I'm supposed to be grateful," he said.

And then I said — God knows what got into me, probably the drink, but it was more than that, I simply can't resist a dare — I said, "What are you actually jealous of?"

He really did seem perplexed. "What are you talking about?" he asked.

"You know what I'm talking about." Because I knew that he knew I had seen him staring at young Mr. Curtis.

And suddenly he zeroed in — he's never actually done this before — and in a split second his hands were around my neck and I thought he was going to strangle me. "Don't you ever! Don't you ever imply something like that again!" I struggled to speak but I couldn't actually because he was strangling me, and for a moment he started to lift up my dress and I thought he's going to rape me and strangle me at the same time, which oddly enough was not an unappealing notion in a bizarre way.

But then he let me go and left, just like that.

And I fell to the floor because, well, I was choking and very weak.

What does this all mean? It means that he has now managed to make me actually afraid of him and myself — which is the worst part of it all. And so, when he starts rewriting the script to reflect this it makes me very uncomfortable, but also oddly excited. I don't enjoy the confusion between art and life.

I met an old lesbian once. I know that makes me sound terribly debauched, but really, at the time I didn't ever really know what a lesbian *was*, and after I met her I explained to one of my friends that I had met a woman who had sex with women and my friend said, "Oh, that's what they call a lesbian." And I said, "I always thought that being a lesbian meant that you like to have sex with two men at a time." I honestly did think that. Well, no, it turns out that lesbians have sex with women, and this woman was a lesbian. And under her suit — she was wearing a man's suit — she had on a leather bra, which I coveted, and she told me she just adored tying up beautiful young women and watching them squirm. This fascinated me, but also the question of physical danger raised its ugly head. "Oh, we have a *safe word*," she said. "I always give my girls a safe word."

"What does that mean?" I asked.

"Oh, I give them a word, and if she says that word then I stop."

"Oh, that's nice of you," I said.

"Yes," she said. "Sometimes too nice."

I asked her what she meant by that and she said, "Sometimes it's better without any safe words at all."

Wow, I thought to myself. And that just makes me think about Nick and me, and this damn movie, and, well, everything.

* * * * * *

So I will say it. There is a young man in my Shakespeare poetry class. Hence my obsession of late with *Venus and Adonis*. I can't quite believe that he is in my class, and that's for a very good reason; he's not supposed to be. His name is Pierre LeRoi, which means Pierre the king. He took this same class of mine a year and a half ago. And I failed him. I noticed him very much in that previous class. He bears a bizarre and uncanny resemblance to Marky Mark. (In the old days, before Marky Mark became Mark Wahlberg, when he was just a beautiful boy.) And he likes to wear a toque to class. And then his arms — oh dear.

But I won't go on. I think you get the picture. I will just mention the soft purity of his skin and the solid squareness of his manly hands. And his certainty. There, I've said enough. So when Pierre was registered in the class previously, I failed him because he hardly showed up at all.

When he did, I was mesmerized by him. There was something very precise about the way he answered questions, and I noticed that he liked to use very flowery academic language, although he hadn't completely mastered it yet. He was like a charming ghost of poetry who would materialize in my class now and then, bewitch me, and then disappear. Occasionally he would ask questions. And once or twice he wore a leather jacket to school. This I found fascinating. Do leather jackets really mean anything anymore? I mean, when I was a child they used to mean homosexual, but I'm sure it's not the same thing these days. After James Dean and Marlon Brando all that is over, I would expect. Nevertheless, the other boys rarely wear leather jackets, but there was Pierre in one. He attended so few classes that it was impossible to pass him. I don't think he even turned in his final exam.

Anyway, I tried to forget about him. I really did. Then, approximately a year later, I saw his name on the list for another iteration of the same class. This perplexed me as it makes absolutely no sense for students to take the same class twice. The course was not *required*. I emailed him about this, asking him why he would want to sit through the same lectures for a second time. He said that was no problem. When he returned for the second iteration, I noticed that he hadn't changed too much; his good looks had simply solidified, and he was as irresistibly boyish as ever. Now he attended every class and contributed quite regularly and intelligently to the discussion. But it seemed to me that now and then when he made a comment in class, he would look at me rather intently. I don't know even if *intently* is the right word. He would look me right in the eye, and it would seem that he was appealing to me in some way. That is, searching my eyes for *something*. Was he simply looking for approval? Again, there might not have been anything in this. But then he began sitting down right beside me every class. It began to concern me because I like to stretch out my feet — I have arthritis — and I was concerned that my feet might touch his by accident. And because of my developing neuropathy (deadened nerves in my feet) it was also quite possible that my feet might touch his without my knowing it. He was always emailing me with questions about the assignments, and then one day he made some sort of a mistake — sent me the wrong document or wrong assignment or whatever — and he wanted to apologize, and he asked if he could go to Tim Hortons and buy me a doughnut and a coffee to apologize. I told him that I didn't like doughnuts (they are not good for my figure) but that a coffee would be fine, and then he asked me how I like it. This question, in the midst of my obsession with him, seemed somewhat pornographic, but I said, "Double double" — which was a lie because I just couldn't bear to say these two words out loud to him: "Double cream." There was a gigantic coffee waiting for me in class. I made the mistake of thanking him for it in front of the rest of the students. It felt awkward.

Also, I must take a bus to school because I never learned to drive. It wasn't until halfway through the semester that I realized that he was on it. This terrified me because I certainly didn't want to talk to him. He did refer to it once, in front of the whole class. "What a traffic jam when we were taking the bus today, eh?" and I was embarrassed because then the whole class knew that we were taking the same bus. And, finally, one day at end of term I was preparing to leave, and my sweater was on the back of the chair. I turned away for a moment to talk to some students, and when I turned back the sweater was gone. Pierre was gone, too. I turned to the students: "Have you seen my sweater?" I asked. One of the students, referring to my much remarked upon absent-mindedness, said, "If you go back to your office it's probably there. You probably just didn't bring it." But I went back to my office and it wasn't there. At the end of the semester Pierre received a very high mark, which he definitely deserved. But did he steal my sweater? I have to admit that it did occur to me that he — well what am I to think? Of course not.

I went home immediately and watched two Joan Crawford movies. I have a pile of old videotapes and an old video machine (which I know is desperately antique), and when I'm in any sort of state, but not in the mood to be Gloria, I put something on. The status of the actress — as actress — that I choose to view lies in direct relationship to my personal distress. When I have lost all reason, I will watch, let's say, Anne Baxter or Lana Turner. (My old TV set is visible from the bay window, and I am so embarrassed by what I watch that I take great care in closing the curtains tightly.) When I'm feeling rather better about myself, but still not good, I will put on Joan Crawford. When I am feeling better still but not quite creative and functional, I will watch Barbara Stanwyck, Bette Davis, or — you guessed it — Gloria Grahame. (Especially *In a Lonely Place* — my favourite of all her movies — Nicholas Ray's terrifying classic film noir portrait of a woman who falls in love with a man who seems to be a murderer.) That my obsessing over the missing sweater that day led me to Joan Crawford — well, it says something about the degree of my upset.

But this is craziness. It's all insane. And I must put it all aside. I pray that I will not see that young man again, ever, in the real world. Especially not two years from now, or later.

Because then I will feel I have the licence to — submit myself to him.

It isn't that I am insulted, it isn't that he has hurt me, it isn't that I am crying. I am certainly not crying over all this. I couldn't even be bothered to cry at this moment, over Nicholas Ray. But things have changed, irrevocably, inevitably I guess, and there is no redeeming him or me or this situation, and that's the way it goes. And it's not because I'm afraid of being abused. I know exactly how much he has abused me and how much it has aroused me, and I am not ashamed to say it. You just try and make me ashamed, I dare you. I, Gloria Grahame, am not ashamed of anything. I would rather die; honestly, I would rather die than be ashamed. So it's not about that. It's about what I finally discovered about him — my husband — who is now my husband in name only. So we were rehearsing one of the scenes from *In a Lonely Place*, and it was, of course, in our living room, which in itself is surrealistic.

Did I tell you that he has not only reproduced the flowered curtains in our house for the set, and in my trailer, but he has arranged the living room in the movie so it resembles ours? It's details like this that make me think he is "gaslighting" me and the purpose is to drive me mad. Well, forget it, darling, you won't succeed! I can't be driven mad, and I'm not a heroine in a nineteenth-century melodrama. The scene was one in which Laurel tries as best she can — without hurting him or turning against him — to drill Dixon about the night of the murder. I was playing the scene as honestly as I could and focusing on intention, a technique that I learned from my mother. I read one section several times with him and he would say, just as he always does, "Again" each time, not actually telling me what was wrong with my reading. Which is infuriating. He finally threw the script down and started pacing on the other side of the room. "Are you constitution-ally incapable of playing a good woman?"

So he was on to this again.

"Oh, please, just shut up," I said.

"It's not in your contract to say that to me," he said.

"I don't care," I said, and lit a cigarette. At first it just seemed boring, him going on like this. "Go ahead and fire me if you want." I knew he wasn't going to fire me, just try and make my life miserable. Well, let him try.

"Well, you wouldn't know what I'm talking about by asking you to play good, would you?" was his rhetorical question. "Because you're constitutionally incapable of it, it seems!"

"I'm not going to *play* good," I said. "You don't *play* good, that would be indicating, and I'm not going to indicate."

"Okay. I'll ask the question in another way."

"I'm really not interested in this question," I said.

"Let me ask you, are you actually capable of speaking to a man without flirting with him?"

"I don't know what you mean," I said, and truly I didn't know.

"There you go." He threw up his arms in frustration, sat down on the chair, put his head in his hands, tried to ruffle his hair — which is too tightly curled to ruffle, so he only succeeded in messing it up, making him look more unhinged. Then he raised his head, and stared at me intently. "That's the problem with you. You're incapable of talking to a man and not flirting. How many times do I have to tell you that this woman never flirts?"

"All women flirt, all the time."

"No they don't. A *good* woman doesn't."

"So you're saying that I'm an irredeemable whore?" I thought that was *quite* brilliant.

"I'm saying that you don't know what a good woman is, because you're not one and you never will be."

Again, I wasn't even shocked or hurt, just flabbergasted, not because he was so obviously manipulating me, because unfortunately he was trying very hard to do so but failing. His technique of humiliating me had backfired and he was revealing something about himself that he couldn't take back, and it seemed to me that I finally understood where he was coming from and it was appalling. He settled in. "You see, it seems to me, Gloria, that since you *do* use the Stanislavsky technique, and since you do play from yourself and your own personal feelings, that if you had a good woman in you, then you could play one. But since you don't seem to be able to access a good woman inside of you, then you must not be a good woman at all, deep down. And it seems that I have made a mistake in casting."

"I told you, go ahead, fire me," I said.

"Well I'll be damned if I'm going to let you turn in another one of your pouting performances." He stood up and shrieked at me, flailing his arms about, uncontrollably. "Stop your pouting! Stop your fucking pouting! There's nothing to fucking pout about! Do you hear me?"

"I'll pout if I damn well want to," I said. "You leave my pout out of this." But suddenly it was all revealed to me. Nick had hinted so many times that I was a whore, and it never hurt me; to his chagrin and my pleasure, it simply aroused me.

Now I finally understood what precisely was making him so mad about my performance in this movie and my performance in his life: *my desire.*

And that, of course, included my desire for him. In a flash he became more than detestable, I hated him to the core, because he wanted to make me ashamed of who I was. No betrayal is more fundamental than that. I picked up the script and I honestly felt that if I read the script the way he wanted me to, he would have been bored out of his mind, and that would have proved my point, and maybe this moment between us, and our whole marriage, could have been saved. I read the scene with him. I didn't do anything but read the lines with intent. I wasn't anyone. I wasn't Gloria Grahame. I wasn't even a woman — which is certainly impossible, but I was as far away from a woman as I was capable of being.

"Well that was fucking boring," I said, tossing the script on the couch. And then he slapped me. Just like that, he slapped me. Hard. It made my jaw throb.

"You whore," he said. And then he walked out of the room. I didn't cry; I wasn't shattered; I didn't burst into tears.

I, Gloria Grahame, was not capable of being ashamed then, nor is it possible for me now, or at any time in the future.

What was much more frightening to me was that I had now permanently come to understand something horrible about the man who at one point had been my very real husband. He actually would have preferred it if I were to divest myself of my desire and become a woman without want, a woman without needs. It was such a startling and repulsive revelation that I knew it would never go away. It was like witnessing a grotesque disfiguring car accident; it was like coming across the steaming, wrenched, distorted limbs of the recently dead. I will never be able to get it out of my mind.

There was some difficulty with the grant for my production of *Venus and Adonis*. I applied almost three months ago, and the arts council told me that I would receive my results at this time. I have not. I called them. When I called, the very polite woman in charge of the theatre section said that three of the jurors had some questions they wished to ask me about my application. I asked her if this was usual procedure, and she said, candidly, that no, it wasn't. She seemed to be speaking honestly with me about a situation that was, to her, as odd as it was to me.

I asked her: "What is the problem?"

And she was quick to say: "There is no problem at all, *per se*," — she used the quaint expression *per se* and then paused. "The jurors would simply like to ask you some questions."

This didn't sound like regular procedure to me at all. "I really don't understand," I said.

"They wish to clarify things."

"What do they wish to clarify?"

"They said that the grant brought up certain issues for them."

"Issues?" I asked. "What ... issues?"

"It really would be better if they talked to you in person, and they have asked to meet with you."

"I have to meet with three people about my grant?"

"Yes, if you wouldn't mind," she said, sweetly and calmly.

"Separately or together?"

"Separately," she said, gently. "Each of them has slightly different concerns."

"It seems like an awful lot of trouble. I'm not the only one who has been asked to answer questions about my work, I presume?"

"No, certainly not. I want to make that perfectly clear." Now she seemed a little less candid; it seemed possible that she was reading from some sort of script.

"And what if I don't want to answer them?" I really was getting quite annoyed.

"Well, in that case, they did ask me to inform you that if you did not co-operate with them and answer their questions, then it might hurt the chances of your getting a grant."

Well, that was subtextually unequivocal. "And if I do meet with them?"

"It is possible you might get your grant."

"How possible?"

"It would not be impossible." Well, that was certainly clear enough. I thought of *Venus and Adonis*, and, most of all, I thought of the beautiful young boy who might play Venus. Maybe it would be Pierre LeRoi, who, after all, had been an acting student as well in the theatre program. Maybe I would meet him and it would be two years from the time that he was in my class, and he would want to star in my *Venus and Adonis*, and confess his obsession with me, and show me the sweater he had stolen from me, so long ago.

"All right, let's set up these meetings then."

The woman was gracious and somewhat apologetic after that. It appeared she was caught in the web of something larger than her. Something that she herself clearly didn't understand. But she was following orders. I saw no need to blame the messenger. I made the necessary appointments.

* * * * * *

I was in our kitchen on a sunny day, the cheerful rays pouring in from under the Spanish-style roof, fixing some breakfast for Timmy, which just means heating baby food. But it has to be warmed to exactly the right temperature. There was a knock on the door. Looking back on it now, it was so touching that he knocked, and also somewhat terrifying, if you consider that it was his own house. For surely he would have realized that Nick was at work. There is a code to the front gate; he had it.

I approached the door, flustered; no one knocks on the door of a Hollywood home during the day, everything is delivered at a specific time, and they know the code. I was wearing an apron, so I must have looked more housewife-like than ever. And, indeed, I am a housewife, any way you look at it. I remember I had a glance in the mirror and all seemed perfectly correct; I had a little lip treatment the day before, and my lips were firm and poutable, my blond bob hanging just below the ears — casual yet responsive (I caressed it and there was a little bounce) — and my eyes were (as always, my best feature) mysterious, and with their slightly hooded quality, bewitching. I know it sounds terribly vain of me to always check before opening the door, but you never know, there are fans everywhere — one might have scaled the fence — and it's important to give them what they want, as they pay the bills.

Well I opened the door, and I remember I was brushing some crumbs off my apron because I had noticed there was residue from a piece of toast, and I looked up and there he was. I quickly raised my eyes so as not to be giving him the fellatio look; I want you to understand that I was painfully aware that he was just a boy and that I was his stepmother.

He had certainly grown quite a bit in the ten months since we had last seen him, but that sometimes happens to boys, they have a sudden spurt. Looking at his eyes, I immediately noticed something. They are not exactly piercing, but they do look right into you, they are small but direct, and under a heavy brow. His eyes were appealing to me with a directness that was impossible to ignore.

He was wearing his school uniform — a military outfit of some kind — and he looked dashing in it. Yes, *dashing* would be the word. I said, "Tony," and gushed in a motherly way and gave him a motherly hug. I really did feel terribly bad that he had felt it necessary to knock. "You didn't need to knock."

"I thought maybe Dad would be here," he said, peering around.

"No, he's not. He's at the studio," I said, and I saw Tony visibly relax. It's important for me to tell you now — it's important for you to understand what Nick did to him. Though Tony had, at first, complained of his father's excessive "fatherliness" and his increasing "avuncularity" (Tony called it "Dad acting like a Dad again") it was much more than that. Nick treats him with a base sort of indignity that is impossible for me to understand, and the reason is clear to anyone with two eyes. Nick is threatened by his son; completely threatened.

And why would that be? I hesitate to speculate. The most innocent explanation would be that Tony is quite obviously brilliant, probably talented, and I think he will be a film director someday. Once, when he was only twelve, he was looking at some sort of avant-garde movie magazine from Europe that Nick had left lying around and he had the temerity to ask Nick if he'd ever heard of Kenneth Anger. Apparently, Kenneth Anger is some experimental director that Nick doesn't approve of. I don't see why Nick shouldn't approve of him; he is always going on about cinematic experimentation. This was only a few months after Timmy was born, so I was in the kitchen feeding him, and just as I was aiming the baby spoon toward his baby mouth, pretending actually that it was a little airplane, which made my little baby smile, I could hear voices raised in the living room. "And what were you doing reading that?"

And I heard Tony's boyish tones: "It was lying around."

"So did I give you permission to read anything that's lying around?"

"No, but —"

"Don't say that to me. Don't say that to your father." I heard a scuffle and I knew that Nick had grabbed ahold of him, bully that he is. Honestly, I'm so glad we don't have a dog, because if we did, Nick would kick it.

It was so obvious that Nick's abuse was confusing and strange to his son. I knew that during these last two years Tony had watched his father not only become more of an alcoholic and a dedicated gambler, but also speak down to his son as if he was even more of a child than when he was a baby. However, now he was seeing his father turn into a dangerous adversary, someone who would turn fiercely angry at him for no reason. I could see Tony's eyes in my mind's eye, like a frightened animal, looking up at his father, terrified and bewildered. I had to go to the door and peer in. Sure enough, Nick had a hold of his arm, and was squeezing it, uncomfortably. "Ow. That hurts."

"You're damn right it hurts. Keep your fucking nose out of *Film Forum*."

"But I like that stuff."

Nick pressed harder with his grasp and was able to shake the boy with his one hand. "You like *Film Forum*, eh? You like reading about Kenneth Anger?"

Tony, god bless him, didn't back down. "Yes, I do." He wasn't exactly fiercely defiant, but he had said it at least, looking right into his father's eyes, disbelieving. "I don't understand. I thought ... you liked that magazine and —"

"I don't care what you think." He let go of Tony's arm. Tony rubbed it.

"Stop being such a fucking sissy," Nick said. "Listen to me. Kenneth Anger is a fucking pervert and he's not even a filmmaker at all, so you can stop reading stupid articles about him."

"But —"

"Don't 'but' me —" I could tell Nick was on the verge of making an off-colour joke. "You want to be a filmmaker? Is that what you're telling me?" He picked up the lighter from a table and lit a cigarette and wandered around the room. He really was acting like a bull, strutting around and puffing up his manly chest as if the whole business of dressing his son down turned him on in some way.

"Well, I was thinking …" ventured Tony.

"Yeah, well, don't think. I told you to stop thinking. You're not going to become a goddamned filmmaker. Do you think it's a nice life? Do you want to end up like your father?"

"Well, Dad, I —"

"I'm telling you, you don't. Do you hear me?"

Tony opened his mouth.

"Don't think, don't speak, just shut up. And I don't want to hear anything about Kenneth fucking Anger and his perverted porno films." Nick stood up and threw the magazine in the garbage can. "Do you hear me?"

"Yeah, I hear you."

"Okay. Jesus." Then Nick turned and he saw me. "What do you think you're looking at?"

I went back into the kitchen to feed the baby. Not because I was afraid to confront my husband — never that — more because I didn't want to fight with him in front of Tony.

The next day, after spending most of the night out gambling and partying, Nick called me into the bedroom. He was sitting on the bed in his bathrobe, smoking; he started to talk about sending Tony to military school. He said that Hollywood was a bad influence and, more than that, *he* was a bad influence and he didn't want his boy growing up to be like his father. It was difficult to know what to say. It's pretty difficult for anyone to be a good father when they obviously hate themselves. I knew Tony would detest military school.

He wasn't the "sissy" that his father called him, but he was bookish and sensitive, and he didn't need disciplining; in fact, the opposite. I felt so sorry for Tony and opposed his idea. But the thing about Nick is that the more you fight with him, the more stubborn he gets — so I realized it was best to drop the subject and pray it would disappear into the miasma of booze and pills that seemed to be engulfing him at that time.

Nick goes through phases — in some of those phases he is drinking more heavily than others. The only thing that saved him really was that after he sent Tony off to military school he just stopped drinking altogether for a while. He was almost a pleasant human being for a brief time. But it didn't last; he started going crazy as soon as we started filming.

So knowing his history with his father, and remembering Nick's recent abuse of me — well, when I saw Tony in his military uniform and his suitcases on the doorstep it was all I could do not to kiss him on the lips. Of course I wanted to comfort him, but I also wanted to share with him a bond that I knew we both had, a bond that was, at its core, a reaction to Nick's abuse. I felt feelings for him that were very deep. It was confusing to me though, because although I assumed the feelings were motherly — and certainly they were — I was worried about Tony's relationship with Nick. And at the same time, I was worried about my own relationship with my husband. In this way, Tony and I had become — in my mind — not stepmother and stepson, but twins. So when he sat down on the couch as I went into the kitchen to fix him a cup of coffee, after putting the baby back in his crib, I was brimful of something — and that something was anticipation. Yes, that's what it was. I had so much to say to him. I was overflowing.

I came home after my first visit to the arts council, and immediately I felt the need to write Gloria. I felt confused and terrible; but I also needed to really disappear, not just watch an old movie. The visit had been nerve-racking from the start. It's amazing how inhospitable those arts council offices can be. It seemed to me as if the environment was calculated to intimidate.

The room was rather small, with no windows, just a long institutional table and two chairs facing each other. And there was only one decoration on the wall, a print of a painting by Kent Monkman — of himself, dressed in drag as Miss Chief Eagle Testickle. In the painting, Miss Chief Eagle Testickle reclines meditatively, floating through the clouds. A pale pink fabric barely covers her resplendent nakedness. Enigmatically, her arm encircles a huge bald eagle; not so enigmatically, she sports a pair of red and black high heels. Her beautiful long black hair flows behind her, tossed by a capricious wind. I was comforted by the painting; surely this was a good sign.

The door opened and I immediately stood at attention. A "being" entered. They were obviously what is lately called a "they." To me, the being appeared to be a man in a dress, as they were quite masculine in their movements and had a full five o'clock shadow, and they were not wearing any feminine makeup. However, they *were* sporting a delicate white blouse and floor-length, flowing skirt, decorated with a bright floral, tropical print. I tried to relieve what to me was the obvious tension emanating from my person: I said, "Hello" and introduced myself.

They said that they were pleased to meet me and then said: "My name is Bee — that's *B*, then *E*, then *E*. And my pronoun is 'they.'"

"Ahh," I said.

"And your pronouns?" they asked, with a courteous tilt of the head.

"Oh, I'm a 'he,'" I said, somewhat uncomfortably — realizing the word did little to describe my perennially yielding, vulnerable self. Bee didn't seem to notice, and opened my file. Then we both began to speak at the same time. I apologized. Then there was another pause. Hoping to fill the void with trivial but pleasing conversation, I opined, with a wry smile, "Oh, by the way, I love the Kent Monkman self-portrait."

"We love it, too," said Bee, matter-of-factly. I couldn't help noticing that their voice was obviously male. I still wondered exactly what caused them to identify as a they. But I had learned from university etiquette that it is impolitic to ask.

Another pause. "I'm so glad it's not a Group of Seven painting," I commented, attempting — with idle chat — to find a common ground. "I get so tired of them." I was hoping this would suggest I was an open-minded, modern person. "Did you know that the Group of Seven were theosophists?" I said, for no apparent reason other than to keep the conversation going.

"Pardon me?" said Bee, again, quite politely.

"The Group of Seven were theosophists."

"I don't know what that means," said Bee.

I sensed, intuitively, that this rather academic observation was a non-starter, but I couldn't resist rambling on. "Theosophy was a mystical philosophy, very popular in the late nineteenth century in England and North America." I realized I was lecturing because I was terrified of the situation, and lecturing was something I did every other day at school. "It was a philosophy that taught there were Gods in natural things, in the environment. That God was in a rock, for instance. Their philosophy was somewhat akin to Indigenous philosophy."

As I should have known, this produced no reaction from Bee whatsoever. They cleared their throat and took a moment to examine my file. "So, we wanted to ask you some questions about your very interesting application." It occurred to me that "we" might refer to Bee, or it might refer to the arts council as a whole. "We must ask you not to feel as if you are on trial. The fact is that it is precisely those projects that inspire questions that sometimes prove to be the most fundable."

"Yes?" I said, hopefully. Despite their best efforts, I was not fully convinced. "What, particularly, did you wish to ask?"

"Well" — they checked something in my file, and then continued — "your project certainly does raise questions about gender. Ones that, of course, could be best answered by you alone. For we wish to give you a fighting chance." They made a cute little fist.

"And what kind of questions does it raise about gender, exactly?" I asked. I did not want to challenge them.

"Well, in your version of *Venus and Adonis*, you have proposed to have a young man play a woman."

"Yes." And since Bee seemed to have paused, I continued, "It's a radical notion, I know, because I'm interested in the masculinity of Venus, and also I'm hoping to do a completely queer reading of —"

"If you'll excuse me," said Bee — there was nothing adversarial, or aggressive about the interruption — "you are suggesting that a cisgendered man would be playing a cisgendered woman. Have I got that right?" Again, their manner was non-threatening — but nevertheless the specificity of the query struck terror in my heart.

"Yes," I said, hoping I had not committed a mortal sin.

Bee continued: "We don't entirely understand what the gender status of the person would be who is playing the role of the woman. Would they be a female impersonator, a trans person, or — what?"

They were, in fact, pouring out a puddle for me to step in. I should have known; but how could I? Looking back on it, I could obviously have suggested that the young actor would be a trans person, but it was, in fact, not something I would ever think of — and even if I had anticipated Bee's objections and tried to improvise, I would have been quite out of my depth.

I simply thought that I might as well be honest. "Well, I was thinking," I offered tentatively, "that it would be a young man who perhaps had some experience in performing in drag."

There was a pause. "Drag?" asked Bee.

"Yes, drag," I said.

Bee appeared to wince, visibly. It seemed to me that I might have uttered what was — to some at least — a dirty word. Bee spoke slowly and deliberately, "I am trying to help you here. I am honestly trying to help you" — and I did honestly believe they were, despite the fact that the being who was sitting in front of me obviously found any mention of drag disgusting. They spoke carefully, "You realize that drag is problematic for some?"

I hoped Bee did not notice my helpless wonder at their remark. I knew that drag queens were disapproved of by hardline "lesbian feminists who wore plaid" back in the eighties, but as I had been somewhat out of the "scene" for many years, I was shocked to see they were disapproved of again — especially by a man who was *himself* wearing a dress.

As if to try and reassure me, they said, "Perhaps I should specify: *some on the jury* find it problematic." It didn't really matter though, because Bee's consistent use of the third person plural pronoun had made it impossible for me to distinguish if they were speaking for themselves or a disapproving quorum. "You see, the problem for trans people," they said gently, "like myself, is that drag often appears to be parodying or making fun of trans people, who are, of course, in earnest about their identities, which they take very seriously, and must deal with day to day, unlike drag queens who get dressed up only occasionally to have a party or — perform. Thus, drag can be very hurtful for some trans people."

All this was beyond my ken. To me, it had always seemed odd that some might find drag cruel or insensitive, as the boys who perform in drag are often quite feminine, bruised creatures themselves. And though I would have expected to cast a very beautiful feminine boy as Venus, I had not imagined him actually doing a drag performance. I simply wanted to mention that the young actor in my play might be one who had experience as a drag queen. But none of this mattered; it had obviously been absolutely the wrong thing to say. I didn't know what to do. Somewhat recklessly, I then tried to gently contest their assertion, which was precisely the wrong thing to do. "I don't really understand why some might find drag offensive — that is, in this modern day and age, what with the popularity of RuPaul?" This was my fatal mistake. I had tried to give my declarative sentence an upward "valley girl" tilt — as my female students so often did — so as to be unthreatening, but it did not work.

Bee closed the file, with a lethal slowness. They spoke as a fair-minded judge might, when sentencing a very nice person to electrocution. "I'm sorry to hear you mention RuPaul. Are you not aware of what RuPaul said when he was asked how he felt about transgender persons appearing on his show?"

Of course, I had no idea what they were talking about, or why I had made such a heinous error by mentioning RuPaul's

name. I had thought RuPaul was "hip" and contemporary —
after all, my students all seemed to love him. "No," I stum-
bled. "I'm sorry, I'm not aware of —"

Bee rose to their full height as their voluminous skirt fell
gracefully to the floor. I realized the skirt was — among, of
course, other things — a calculated dramatic effect. "RuPaul
has made quite clear his disdain for trans people. He would
not allow certain trans people on his program, stating, and
I quote: 'You can identify as a woman and say you're transitioning, but it changes once you start changing your body.'"

I was certainly very impressed they could quote RuPaul
verbatim, but I also knew this was the end for me — at the
very least with Bee. "Something for you to think about." They
turned slowly, and it appeared to me, a little sadly.

"Is that all you wanted to ask me?" I asked them — before
they touched the doorknob. I couldn't stop the helpless plead-
ing in my voice.

They turned to me, slowly but kindly. "Yes. For now."

And they were gone.

I was coming back from the kitchen with some coffee; I had
made him coffee. I think it was partially to gain time and
gather my thoughts. But coffee also seems like such an adult
thing to drink. Tony was nearly fourteen. He certainly looked

much older than his age, and it wasn't just the growth spurt. His face had become distinctly triangular — it had lost all the roundness of a child and was slender, like the head of a young deer. It was actually a V shape, with his strong brow forming a straight line at the top of it. And I couldn't help noticing the back of his neck. In fact, it obsessed me. He had a military-style haircut, but — had the barber made a mistake? — there was a trail of full, dark hair down the back of his neck. It was like the neck of a wild animal. It was almost feral, and it seemed to belie his youth.

Despite myself, I couldn't help thinking of that moment last year when his door had been open and I had seen what I shouldn't have.

I sat down opposite him on the sofa. The living room, which now reminded me of the set for *In a Lonely Place* (when it should have been the other way around) was very cozy — not only with the floral-patterned curtains but also the paintings of women, both prints, one by Manet and one by Van Gogh. They made the room feminine and friendly, a feeling I wanted the room to have. However, Tony sat right next to a lamp that had always made me somewhat uncomfortable — the body of it is somewhat oddly shaped, like a pineapple, with oddly pointing, protruding leaves that are slightly threatening. It was the one article in the room that Nick had chosen. And one of the paintings was, unfortunately, slightly crooked, but I didn't bother to straighten it.

We drank our coffee together. He sat very erect in his school uniform. I felt sorry for him; there was no need for

Tony to be at a military school. It completely served his father's need to get rid of him — and Tony's needs not at all.

"So how are things?" I asked.

"Well …" he looked down at his coffee cup. I realized that Tony's voice had changed. I don't know why I hadn't noticed it before. Perhaps his voice sounded higher in the clear light of day on the front porch. Or maybe it was that inside the house there was less competing noise. It wasn't terribly deep, but it was lower and soft, gentle. "Things are all right," he said.

But clearly, they weren't. "Is military school as bad as you thought it would be?" I asked, trying to understand how distressed he really was by military school, and at the same time make light of the situation.

"Pretty much," he said, without humour. And then he quickly changed the subject to what was obviously on his mind. "How's Dad?"

I didn't want to answer. That is, I wanted to say it all, to say everything I was feeling about his father, but I knew it wouldn't be appropriate. "Not so good," I said, putting down the coffee.

"Is he drinking?" asked Tony.

"Yes, he's drinking, and doing other things."

"Oh, God," said Tony, his voice catching in a way that made me think him a boy again. He gulped. "Do you think he wants me here?"

I used my best soothing tone. "He's been talking about it. I think he's looking forward to your visit." This was a lie.

Christ. I didn't want to lie. I wanted to protect him. I could tell that Tony was frightened.

But what touched me was that he turned from his own feelings and expressed concern for me. "And how are you doing?" he asked. How different he was from Nick. How different and similar at the same time. Tony had all of Nick's animal magnetism, it was there, I could see it, at a distance, without succumbing to it, surely — but instead of Nick's edge he had no edge at all. He was gentle, kind, yet still effortlessly masculine.

"How am *I* doing? Why do you ask?" His kindness overwhelmed me so much that I was stalling.

He would have none of it. "I want to know about you. Is he treating you all right?"

This question was admitting to so much. We had never openly spoken of Nick's abuse, and now we were dangerously close to talking about it. A part of me felt that I shouldn't accept his concern, that he was just a boy and shouldn't worry about me, but another part of me was desperate for his sympathy. I couldn't tell anyone else about the way Nick treated me. Does that sound crazy? Well how was I to actually tell people about it? First of all, it would destroy his career if I spread it around that he was a drunk and a drug addict. But the more frustrating thing was that even my few female friends would never understand. They would have made me feel awful for loving Nick. And they would accuse me — I know it — of somehow being complicit in my abuse. But I was just being a woman, and honestly desiring him.

And despite recent violent encounters with Nick, I wasn't ready to admit to myself that our marriage was disintegrating. I couldn't stand the pity, I couldn't stand the condescension of those prying eyes, and — I know this sounds ridiculous — but I just couldn't stand having made a life choice that was so wrong.

When you choose someone — and certainly when you have a child with them — it's not easy, at least for someone like me, to start whining about what a beast the man is. And this was the essence of my bond with Tony. Tony was the only other person I knew who understood how horrible Nick could be, and, like Tony, I was saddled with him. Out of a strange necessity, we both had this beast in our lives and neither of us could rid ourselves of his presence. But even though I wanted to spill all of this in Tony's lap, I didn't feel I should. It would be wrong. Wouldn't it? I knew that sharing these feelings with Tony would be dangerous, and not at all the right protocol for a stepmother and her stepchild — but then again, what about this entire situation was in any way normal? In what respect were we actually a family? Damn it! Why should we follow the rules of a normal family when we were so decidedly not normal, when we were both living in fear of his violent father, who was also my violent husband? Then the door opened. It was Nick — so unexpectedly, during the day.

*　　*　　*　　*　　*　　*

I was somewhat daunted. And this was only the first meeting. But I am anything if not persistent. This is an aspect of my character that I think has served me well over the years; that is, I am still here. I am persistent in the sense that even though I know my presence is blindingly irrelevant to some, that I am irksome, loathsome, and, certainly to many, increasingly invisible, I am like the cockroach on the carrion; when most are gone, I will still be there.

This reminds me of an image. I have, in my life, occasionally (I will admit it) been prey to back rooms. Back rooms are rooms in gay bars where gay men go — often the unloved, but sometimes merely the drunk and horny — to connect with other gay men in the dark. I only go occasionally, it's my one release.

I certainly do better in the dark. Well, there is often a man there — and I know he must be there often because I so rarely go and he is always there when I am. He is difficult to make out in the pitch blackness but sometimes someone turns their cellphone on (it is not allowed), and I catch a glimpse of people's faces or bodies. This man wears a red cap and is of no discernable age. He has a somewhat plump face with a five o'clock shadow, and he has an odd European-style bag slung over one shoulder. He has often touched me, but to no avail. And it is not for lack of interest on my part. I would go with him — he is tall and might be good looking — but what I've learned over the years I have encountered him (and they have been years) is that he is always unlikely to *continue* touching me. And yet he touches me, on many different occasions, over and over again. I don't know if it is some sort of illness on his part, or just his own odd relationship to me, or does he just have a bad memory? But he will, for instance, caress my leg for a bit and then just stop and walk away. It isn't because I respond to him and scare him off — because I rarely do. It's as if he can only endure a certain amount of contact, and then he reaches his breaking point and must depart. Sometimes I can't bear to stand next to him because I know it is fruitless, other times I let him touch me for a bit. But the point is that if he is anything, he is persistent. He will always be there. He is not wanted, and his existence, in that dark room, is pointless, at least to me, but he will not go away.

And in this way I identify with him. I am not saying that I am going to live for a very long time (who knows?) but as long as I am here, I will persist in — if nothing else — slowly disappearing. So what was obviously a rejection by the arts council didn't really daunt me. It was my due. I expect to be rejected and, in a way, I welcome it. But I wasn't quite ready to give up yet. And if they were willing to give me another interview, as they had originally suggested three, then I would see the three interviews out. Perhaps after the next one I would be able to devise a plan for getting them onside, and my silly project (that probably no one would see) might go on.

Precipitously, there was a phone call the next day for me to meet with someone named Dee Frances. She was obviously a woman; though these days one could never be too sure. When I arrived, the Kent Monkman painting was still on the wall. (Why shouldn't it be? Well, they change these paintings sometimes, like an art gallery.) It upset me; Kent Monkman had been very much on my mind the night before. It had certainly occurred to me that not only had Bee criticized my concept of Venus as drag queen when they had been wearing a dress themselves — but when they scolded me, they had been sitting beside a painting of a drag queen. Should I bring up the obvious contradiction? I certainly didn't want to alienate anyone.

Dee entered in a flash of light and noise and colour; at least it seemed that way. Yes, this was a woman, and obviously very comfortable in her womanliness. She was wearing a very bright dress, with what they used to call an A-line skirt, and she almost twirled when she came in. The skirt seemed to be of a space-age design — were there planets on it, or were they pineapples? It was very colourful. The other thing I noticed about her was her glasses, which were very distinctive, pointy — what used to be called "cat-eye" glasses, very vintage. The addition of the soft light-blue sweater made me realize that her outfit was consistent. She was dressed as if for a 1950s malt shop. It was fetching. Certainly this was not all for me. And then I realized, as she began talking, that she was very feminine and charming and this whole look was typical of her daily routine, and it was not specifically for me or anyone else; it was for the world.

"Well, Dr. Moulton. It's a pleasure to meet you. I've heard so much about you."

I couldn't imagine what she had heard. I was glad though, that though she used my dreadful last name she didn't use my more dreadful first one (for the record, it's Denton). "I don't know how you could have heard about me?" I said.

"Oh, your reputation precedes you," she said, charmingly and, it seemed, warmly. "You must tell me about this application. We were fascinated by it. We haven't ever received an application from you before, and we don't usually receive applications from those in the academic world. Of course, I see that you have the requisite professional theatre experience, though it was many years ago, but that's not the issue. The only issue is really, well — you must tell me more about this project; I find it fascinating — what moved you to propose it?"

She seemed sincere, and I was flattered that she wanted me to talk. "Well, I've been very interested in *Venus and Adonis* for many years. It is one of the least understood of Shakespeare's works and, as you know, it is not a play but —"

"Excuse me!" She waved her little pinky at me. "I'm sorry to interrupt you, but what we're really looking for is your theatrical inspiration, not your intellectual one. Of course, your intellectual ideas are valuable and interesting to those who wish to read your books" — How could I tell her I hadn't written any? She should have known that from my resume — "but I am here to help you, especially when I say that juries sometimes do not look kindly on submissions from professors, who they sometimes think are coming at it from an academic — not a theatrical — perspective. So, if I ask you what *compels* you to do this project, what would you say?"

I was quite dazzled by her. She was very pretty, far prettier than I (not that it needs to be said) and so very poised and charming. So I went to a place that probably I shouldn't have. It seemed to me that if I wasn't to appear a hopeless academic, it might be necessary for me to speak personally, so I did. "Well I must say that the inspiration, as you put it, for this piece is quite personal. I, that is I — well, ever since I have been young, I have never really identified as a male. Perhaps I'm expressing that in the wrong way. I'm a gay man, as you probably perceived, but inside, I've always felt as if I was not a man at all. I mean, I know what my body looks like, I know it's the body of a man, and I don't wish to change that, but inside I have always identified as a woman, or a boy."

"Ah." She smiled and nodded. She even licked her lips. But what Dee had in common with Bee was the glacial impenetrability of her expression. I would have no idea of her sincerity unless she somehow confessed it. "Let me just understand what you are saying here."

"Yes, of course," I said.

"You are not saying that you are a trans person, or that you are thinking of transitioning."

"No, no, I'm not saying that, I want to make —"

She interrupted me again, waving her gently disapproving pinky. "Now, I want you to consider your answer very carefully." Was she talking to me in code? I wished I had known at the time (why was I so stupid?) that she was — it seems to me, looking back on it now — offering me a way out of this muddle.

I probably should have told her I was transgendered. But the truth is that I, of course, am not, and so it just wasn't in my mind to bring that up. Instead I continued trying to explain. "No. I am a gay man, but I feel I have a girl inside, and I've always kind of been a girl."

"Be that as it may." She seemed to be struggling with my admission internally. Just the tiniest pressure in her voice and a twitch in her left eye revealed it. "So even though you identify inside as a girl or a boy, not a man, be that as it may, you are a male and use male pronouns?"

"Yes, that is true ..." I had a feeling I was digging my own grave, but I honestly didn't know what else to say. I know that I lie when I write; it's wonderful to do so. But it is much more difficult — and I think less ethical — for me to do it in person.

"So you are a man, who wants to write a play about a woman, Venus, and her attraction for a young man named Adonis."

"Yes, that's precisely correct," I said.

She continued: "Well, I just wanted to understand that." She wasn't saying it, but I felt like I had missed out quite significantly by not identifying as a trans person. But after all, really, how could I masquerade as one? What if they asked me some personal question about my "transness," and I couldn't answer?

"Well let's talk then about your casting decisions. I'm sure you are aware, with your experience in the theatre, of Rina Fraticelli's report entitled 'The Status of Women in Canadian Theatre,' written in 1982?"

I faked a little, but I did vaguely remember. "That was the ..."

"Yes, the report about the underrepresentation of women in theatre as directors and writers. And of course you know there are just simply fewer parts for women. Always have been, regrettably. And in reference to your project specifically, Shakespeare has written such gorgeous roles, but disproportionately fewer for women. And here you have chosen a female character from a Shakespeare poem to dramatize. And Bee has told me that you would have her played by a young man with drag experience. Is that true?"

"Yes," I said tentatively. Here we were again. This was the sticky wicket and there was no way out.

"I'm interested in your justification for that."

So we were back onto casting again. "Need I have a ...?" I couldn't help glancing again, surreptitiously, at the Kent Monkman painting on the wall (was I looking for support?) — I hoped she wouldn't notice.

"Well, ordinarily we wouldn't interfere, but it's a question of representation. It's a question of a part that was written about and for a woman, that is to be given to a man. And a man of course has none of the lived experience that a woman has. In this sense it is a part that is directly to be taken out of the reach of a woman, and appropriated, therefore depriving a woman of an opportunity to act. Cisgendered men have privilege, and they are not women, and if they write as women then they are usurping the position of women in society and, effectively, erasing them."

Oh dear. She had me in a corner, even more of a corner than Bee. With Bee and Dee coming at me on all sides there was no escape. In a moment of desperation, I took my courage from Miss Chief Eagle Testickle.

"I understand," I said carefully, "that Bee has some objection to drag; they think drag ridicules trans people, which is something that, I have to say" — I swallowed my fear but carried on — "I *must* say, I don't entirely understand, because right there in front of me on the wall is a painting — a beautiful painting, by the way — of Chief Eagle Testickle by Kent Monkman, I believe, in which he portrays himself dressed in drag. So, what I don't understand is —"

"Excuse me." Her demeanour changed. Suddenly, Dee was not as pretty as before; her face was contorted with fierce umbrage. I could see that — like a woman scorned — she was not be toyed with when consumed by wrath. "What *exactly* are you saying?"

Oh dear. Confronted with Dee's anger, I didn't quite now know now what I should be saying. "I just wondered —"

"This is an Indigenous painting, by an Indigenous artist. You can't speak about it the same way as you would speak about your own work."

I couldn't stop myself. "It's just confusing to me because, I think I heard Kent Monkman called himself a drag queen once in a newspaper article ..."

"Stop. *Please* stop." She waved her hands in front of her face and stood up. Yet again, I had unwittingly crossed a very distinct and unwavering line in the sand.

"You are not Indigenous. I am not Indigenous. Neither of us has the right to talk about the Indigenous experience with authority. We don't know what it means. We don't know what embodied experience they have suffered. Kent Monkman is a two-spirited person from a two-spirited tradition, and if you speak of his work as a white gay man, or if you speak for a drag queen, you are not only appropriating that work; you are colonizing it. You are, in fact, committing a kind of atrocity in respect to the work of an artist whose legacy is one of exploitation and abuse. What you are speaking about is a kind of erasure of his work. I would ask you to stop speaking of Kent Monkman's work in this way."

All I could do was apologize. "I'm sorry. I'm terribly sorry. I didn't mean to …" I had risen, when she rose; I now sank abjectly into my chair.

"It's just very important that you don't speak about work that you cannot, because of your colonial privilege, truly understand." She seemed somewhat mollified. Could I touch her with tears? I tried to cry, or look like I was crying; I was lying now — in real life. I lowered my head.

"I'm sorry. I'm deeply, deeply sorry. I don't know how I could ever be more sorry," I said. I peered up at her, secretly, from my bowed brow. I could tell she was melting slightly. I looked down at my old thin hands on the table, which did happen to have patchy, pesky bits of hair on the pale fingers. "I'm more sorry than you can" — I tried to put a catch in my throat. After all, I had once been an actor — "ever imagine."

Then she did something very human; I will never quite forget it. She leaned down and pressed my liver-spotted old hand onto the table with what seemed to be very real concern.

"Please *do think carefully* about what I said, before your next interview." Then she twirled out the door, which seemed to slam with a certain coldness behind her. Yes, the room was very cold, and it was not yet winter.

There was no scene. Nick just came directly from the front door into the living room (there is no hall in our Hollywood bungalow) and — looking somewhat surprised at seeing the two of us together — gave his son a perfunctory nod and said, "Welcome back." Then he said, "I have a lot of work to do," and he disappeared into his study. On the one hand, I think Tony was relieved that his father wasn't angry at him for being there. But he was instantly hurt because it was pretty obvious that his father viewed him as an irritating distraction from working on *In a Lonely Place.*

Having finished our coffees, I took Tony down the hall and to the back of the house and showed him his old room, which we had changed because Nick insisted on moving some of Tony's things into boxes, so that his son would know that he was no longer going to be living with us during military school or after.

I could tell that Nick's fiddling with Tony's precious personal items was upsetting for Tony, who said "You saved the horse? You put the horse somewhere?" It was a metal toy horse that he had loved very much as a child. I couldn't help thinking about his own mane, that trail of fur at the back of his neck. I carefully showed him Timmy, who was sleeping, and then it seemed that the domestic tour was done. I said I was going to take a nap, which seemed, in an odd way, to be revealing too much. Then I went back to our bedroom — which was in the centre of the house — all alone and sat on the bed. It was all suddenly seeming very complicated. I realized that it was going to be difficult to have Tony there. It wasn't difficult before. Before, he was just a boy, and all my erotic attention had been focused on Nick. Now Tony seemed like a man and I was sadly and frustratingly moving further and further away from his father.

Nick came into the bedroom from his office, which was the room behind the living room, shut the door, and asked, emotionlessly, "How long is he staying?"

"Over Christmas," I said. "For a couple of weeks."

"It's very inconvenient," he said.

"He's your son, Nick."

"Don't give me that shit," he said. But he didn't raise his voice. He certainly was as threatening as usual, but I realized that now he would have to keep his voice down when we fought because he didn't want Tony to hear.

"What shit?" I asked.

"I can't deal with you making me feel guilty. Remember he's my son, not yours." As if I was liable to forget that. It was actually one of the primary things on my mind. "I'm just saying that if the movie was going better, which means if *you* were

doing better, I wouldn't be in this mental … state. Anyway …
I'm just saying that it's hard for me to dredge up whatever I'm
supposed to dredge up for him, when I'm under this kind of
pressure. Practically rewriting the damn thing every day and
trying to get you to play a fucking nice woman."

"I see, Nick, it's all my fault."

"Damn right it is, so don't go blaming me. And don't encourage him. If he says I don't have time for him, sympathize
with me, will you? Don't talk behind my back about what a
bad father I am. Could you try not doing that?"

"I won't do that," I said. I realized that it was a tall order
and I didn't know at that very moment if it was possible. In
fact, him asking me specifically to do that just made me want
to confess my feelings to Tony more, especially as it seemed
to me that he might be very sympathetic to them and it might
help him so much to hear them. When Nick left, all I could
think was: what would it have cost him to hug his son? It
would have meant so much to Tony. I collapsed on the bed,
crying. I thought I was crying for Tony; but I think I was crying for the both of us, or perhaps even just for myself.

This was my final chance. After my second trip to the arts
council office I cursed myself for my reckless behaviour. But
I couldn't get Miss Chief Eagle Testicle out of my mind.

And on my third visit, when I opened the door to that horrible room, Kent Monkman's masterpiece greeted me once again. Only this time, it appeared to be speaking directly to me. It really was a masterpiece, and I really loved it, and to me, he did look like a drag queen. I stared into Chief Eagle Testickle's eyes. I had actually met Kent Monkman once, at a university gathering. He barely noticed me (why should he?) but I must say that he was a beautiful, elegant man, and he was kind to me — which no one beautiful almost ever is. Would this kind, elegant man who had the generosity of spirit and humility to portray himself in this incredibly witty and poignant way — if he learned of my work — would he have opposed my drag project? It occurred to me that he might actually like my idea for the play. Perhaps the problem was that although he wasn't here to speak for himself, there were too many here to speak for him.

When the door opened, I was standing. What looked like a tall slender man stood there. What was most odd about him was his hair. It was curly, blond, and piled up high on his head to one side, in a kind of French way. He also wore a long dangly earring on the same side. I noticed immediately that he was extremely effeminate, and I thought for a moment that I had met a fellow traveller. Little did I know. At any rate, there was certainly something very prissy about him; for he gave me a kind of tiny smile and gestured for me to sit down. We sat.

He pulled up his chair close to the table and ceremoniously laid his hands on it. I noticed he was wearing a very ornate ring, which looked as if it might easily catch on something. I hoped he put it on *after* his shirts. He smiled his prissy little smile again. And in that prissy smile, I felt a possible kinship. "My name is Pierce Kearney, and, first of all, I want to acknowledge that we are sitting upon the traditional territories of the Mississaugas of the New Credit First Nation, Anishnabeg, Chippewa, Haudenosaunee, and Wendat Indigenous Peoples, the original nations of this land, who continue to cry out for justice." I was quite impressed by his mastery of all the long and complicated names. "I myself am a transgendered person," he continued. "I identify as genderqueer, and I am Cree, as well as having some privileged blood, Irish and Scottish, in equal amounts. And you are Dr. Denton Moulton, I presume?"

"Yes, that is my name, sir," I said, frozen into a kind of formality.

"No need to be so formal," he said, "we're all friends here. I must say, Dr. Moulton, we are trying our best to find a way to support you. We think your project is interesting but, frankly, and here I am being very frank, your work is terribly unique, which interests us very much, but we have not decided if it is unique *in quite the right way*, or completely unique *enough*." He was beyond glacial, beyond impenetrable. "I have one final question for you, Dr. Moulton. We have interviewed you three times now, and that is the maximum amount of time we are allowed to give you, unfortunately. This will be the last interview. So I want you to think seriously about the questions I am going to ask. This is a big question." I tried to brace myself, and even grabbed the arms of my chair. "Can you tell me what you have done today — this very day — to counterbalance your tremendous privilege and give something back to those who are not as lucky as you are?"

So this was to be the deciding question. I really didn't know how to respond. Did he really believe that I had tremendous privilege? Yes, I was a university professor, but the students generally made fun of me, when they were not laughing at my desperate jokes — and I was treated with tremendous condescension by my colleagues. Did he mean the "privilege" of my salary? It's true, I couldn't pretend I was poor, but due to my thin publishing record, I had never been able to get my salary beyond $80,000. And it would not help to plead that the $80,000 a year was much less than my much more privileged colleagues. I searched desperately for something, anything.

Then I remembered an incident that had occurred a couple of months ago. Admittedly it had not been that very day, but it had actually happened. I had been accosted by an Indigenous street person, who was obviously in a very bad way, his face bloated and pimpled, his eyes red and bleary; evidently drunk. Now this story must be told in the context of my usual behaviour, which I had not done with Pierce. For usually I am just terrified of giving money to any street person, as I am afraid they will beat me up. Even the women. I am, as you can imagine, quite physically weak. Once a bag lady — as we used to call them — followed me for blocks repeating over and over again, "Do you have a quarter do you have a quarter do you have a quarter do you have a quarter?" and I was terrified.

So, despite my misgivings, I gave this very sad, bloated man a twenty-dollar bill — which, considering the fact that he was almost certainly already drunk, was probably not a good idea. But I always remembered this incident — because it was so rare — in which I had actually helped a street person. So it wasn't entirely a lie to mention it. In my frenzy — and now it was a frenzy, this was my last chance — I said: "Just this morning I saw the most unfortunate Indigenous man on the street and I gave him twenty dollars because my heart just went out to him."

Pierce Kearney leaned over the table the way Dee had. "Don't you realize what a privileged, exclusionary thing it is to say something like that? You might as well say, *Some of my best friends are Indigenous.*' Only what you have said is much, much worse." He was, of course, correct. What I had said was insensitive; maybe I didn't deserve government funding after all. I was seized with a dense insecurity. I could feel an oncoming numbing, disabling depression followed by a viewing of an endless succession of Rita Hayworth movies — she really was the worst actress of them all. (What did Orson Welles ever see in her, besides physical beauty? That man must have had very low self-esteem.) I wouldn't get my grant, I would never get my grant, and if I wanted to finance my project, the final and only real dream of my life, I would have to move out of my apartment into a rental shack somewhere. How could this be? I wanted it so badly, and that is my only excuse for what happened next.

My eyes turned back to Miss Chief Eagle Testickle, and she seemed to be speaking to me — as one man with a girl inside might communicate with another. Was it possible to ignore skin colour in this particular case? Was it possible that *inside* both of us were, it seemed to me, equivalent, even twins — beyond blood and even race? That we were, after all, just a pair of drag queens? With Miss Chief Eagle Testickle emboldening me, I was ready to lie. *After all*, I thought to myself, *art is essentially a lie*, and it certainly was time for me to use the only weapon at my disposal: my ingenuity. I was a rat caught in a trap; and I therefore would act like one. I needed to query Pierce first. I paused and looked down. "I notice that you are not umm ... evidently Cree. It must make it difficult for you that people might mistake you for being a white person."

He warmed to this, and I realized that two could play this game. "You are perfectly right." Pierce had a very exact way of speaking, clamping down on every consonant. "I am precisely one-eighth Cree, on my grandmother's side. It is a difficult cross to bear, the fact that I'm so often mistaken for a white person. Some people actually want proof, if you can believe it." He chuckled faintly, as if we were sharing a joke.

"And you don't give it to them?" I had to know the answer to this if my plan was to work.

"The horror is that I am the one most strongly aware of my difference; I feel it inside and have carried the pain of my heritage all my life — it is stamped on the collective unconscious."

I jumped right in. (It was a huge gamble, but why not?) "That is precisely my situation," I said.

"Meaning?" he asked, quite open and interested.

I looked down at the table again, a bit regretfully, playing the part of making a difficult confession. Then I plunged in. "I'm part Black."

"You are? Why didn't you tell us?" He was visibly moved, enthusiastic even. I immediately felt terrible because it seemed that I had opened some door into Pierce's soul. But it was something I was forced by circumstance to do.

"I didn't think it was relevant to my project," I said.

"Well, of course it is," said Pierce. "It is relevant to *every-thing*. Of course, it's naive to attempt to separate an author's identity from the value of his work. Have you always known of your heritage, or have you only recently discovered it?"

"My uncle told me," I said. This was certainly very close to the truth. I have extremely white, almost translucent skin, but the strange, almost unexplainable thing is, I have always, like the rest of my family — quite inexplicably — tanned well. I always tan, never burn. When I was young, we were on vacation with my uncle and I asked him why we Moultons were able to get so dark, with our naturally pale skin. He laughed and said — using long out-of-date British slang — "You have a touch of the tar brush, don't you?" This was proof enough for me. It seemed I was trading my future for what was, after all, a little white lie (in the context, the term seemed all too appropriate).

"And what is your background?"

"My family was escaped slaves, on the underground railroad, a long ways back."

"And what was their portal?"

"Portal?" This was going to be difficult.

"Their route to Canada, you know —"

"Oh ..." this was it. It was the end of my project and my life as an artist. I wasn't an artist, anyway. The whole thing was just a pipe dream and would never come to fruition. I just gave up and I threw it out there — like one throws a steak into a pan. "Uncle Tom's Cabin?" It was the only remotely appropriate Black location I could even think of. But, of course, I realized, immediately after saying it, that it was not an actual location but a fictional place. How ridiculous.

But Pierce seemed surprised in a good way. "Oh yes," he said. "Dresden, Ontario — the escape route of Josiah Henderson — the man who was the model for the character of Uncle Tom in the famous novel, of course. I know of the museum there, and I have been there. Of course."

Pierce softened. He looked at me with true sympathy, and it appeared that there were tears in his eyes. Here was someone who seemed to have experienced deeply the real trauma of prejudice — or at least, that's the way he seemed to me — not just to be saying the required words to keep his job. And I had taken advantage of him. But it couldn't be helped. "Oh it must have been so difficult for you. You've carried around this pain for years?"

I swallowed, and with it I swallowed my pride and my virtue, realizing I was giving it all up for my art. "Yes," I said.

"It's really been very difficult." Well *this* was not lying. I had carried a lot of pain around with me for many years, if, perhaps, for slightly different reasons.

"I know. I sympathize," said Pierce. "I can understand why you might have been shy about revealing your identity — people don't understand, but I do — how difficult it is being a multiracial person. And you understand that the idea that an author's identity is irrelevant to a work of art is a colonialist idea, one that has served the status quo for hundreds of years. I mean it's all very well to talk of 'content' as if it is separate from an artist's lived or embodied experience, but we as audiences and critics are not, and cannot be, neutral when it comes to judging content, as we are ourselves trapped in our own embodied experience. In other words, what is valued is still determined by a white patriarchal culture. That culture will always privilege content that reflects its own values. Only by opening up that closed and racist environment to other voices — the voices of other 'lived experiences' — can we begin to start to hear different stories, which will in turn affect our value systems and make them more equitable. In the current environment, we would have a great deal of difficulty funding a play by a cis white male, as that kind of privilege has for so long shut out — *silenced* — other voices, and our mission right now must be to *make room* for those voices. We would be very delighted to give a platform to a voice such as yours that has clearly experienced trauma and marginalization."

Thankfully, after his oration — which did nothing but make me feel dreadfully guilty — Pierce stood up. "Well, thank you again, for your difficult but significant confession. We will not forget it. I think you have given us absolutely *all* the information we need," he said, and then he warmly shook my hand and swept out of the room, his blond curls dangling and twinkling in the bright lights.

I sat in silence for a moment, marvelling quietly to myself at my own actions, and at the fact that Pierce sounded truly cheerful and more animated than any of the other two inquisitors had been, ever. Why in heavens name hadn't I thought of this before? I gazed up — no longer shy — directly into the eyes of Miss Chief Eagle Testickle. She gazed right back. And amazingly (or was it my imagination?) she was not judging me at all.

So now it's done. It's happened. I can't make sense of it, there is no use trying to make sense of it, I can't. But I refuse to blame myself. I simply refuse. If you want to blame me, go ahead, but I don't give a damn. I've managed to live my life up until now without accepting the irritating small-minded judgments of others, so I don't see why I should begin doing that now. What right does he have to judge me, anyway? But it's not Nick I'm worried about, it's the world. No, it's me — I'm worried about my own judgment of myself.

Where in heaven's name do we get these guilty consciences? Who implants them? And what purpose do they serve? Do they actually stop us from doing anything, or do they just make us feel terrible for things we have already done? There are people who live their lives without guilty consciences at all; they are called psychopaths and sociopaths, or maybe they simply could be called much happier people than you or I. They go about their lives blithely stomping on people and they don't give a damn in hell. I know that doesn't excuse my behaviour but it certainly excuses me from the self-flagellation, which I absolutely refuse to endure. I am not about to accept blame for actions for which I do not deserve to be punished. So there. This is what happened. I'm not ashamed of it because I did nothing wrong.

The boy was not a child. Let them pillory me, let them put me in jail. Oh God, I don't mean that. I don't want to go to jail. The only thing that might save me is that Nick wouldn't dare, would he?

No, of course he wouldn't, no matter how much he threatens — this kind of scandal would ruin his career as well as mine. It's all people would talk about. There would be no Nicholas Ray, Filmmaker, anymore, there would just be … well, I don't want to say it. Because they wouldn't understand. Well, screw them. I understand, and it all makes perfect sense to me. It wasn't wrong and it wasn't even remotely a bad thing to do. It was, in its own way, beautiful, and if you can't see that, if no one can see that, well, I really don't care. Be disgusted if you like. Those who are disgusted by love and sex will be a long time regretting a life they never had; or maybe they won't regret it, which is even worse. No, I'm convinced that moralists live on morality the way chameleons (so they used to think, in olden days) live on air. Beauty and pleasure and happiness are just so incredibly rare that when they happen to you, you must experience them. You must. That's my advice. I can die now. I can die now because I have lived — but I don't intend to die any day soon. So there, moralists.

Yesterday I came home from the studio much earlier than Nick, which often happens. And Tony was there. He's always there; he has no friends, and he has absolutely nothing to do. I have given him books of mine to read. Perhaps they are not suitable for a young man. Not because they are indecent — well, I suppose they are, but not in the sense of being dirty — they just might be considered immoral by, well, stupid people. I gave him *Madame Bovary*, for instance. He seems to like it. I wish I hadn't given him anything. Because it always seems that we should talk about the book he is reading, whatever it is, but I know that if I talk with him then it will all come pouring out. So I don't, which seems cruel. Anyway, I'm drifting around the house, and he is always wearing one of Nick's robes. He didn't have a bathrobe at military school. Apparently they all prance around in their underwear there. It's a wonder the place is not a hotbed of perversion — or maybe it is and Tony doesn't talk about it. Nick had, of course, packed up all of Tony's old clothes. And Nick's robe has Nick's initials on it, which makes it more ironic than you can imagine. The robe just falls on Tony. It just gently falls, the way clothing does on a body that is destined to wear it. I can't describe it. I know I wasn't supposed to notice his lean young chest.

Describing it sounds like pornography and this is not that. But I noticed, okay? Call me human, call me a woman, but I noticed it.

I could tell this was going to drive us completely crazy, this huge weighty silence that was hanging over everything, making it impossible to move or think. Because the silence contained all the things we wanted to say to each other about Nick. And so I was the cause of it. I was the catalyst and it's all my fault, because I couldn't stand it anymore, and I wanted to help him. I mean, he hadn't talked to Nick since he arrived back home and practically the only words that Nick had addressed to him were to say "Welcome back." I had tried to confront Nick about it during the first week, but he just got furious and at one point threatened to hit me in a way which, I am sad to say, was not sexy at all; it was just nuts. He just seemed like a crazy man to me all of a sudden. Why don't you want to speak to your own son who has come from miles away just to see you? And do you have any idea what this is doing to the boy?

Well, I think Nick did — or maybe he didn't, it's hard to say, he's so wrapped up in himself and his own problems, not that it makes any difference, anyway, he's simply unavailable to both of us. And I can put up with it, I put up with it all the time. I've never been so lonely in a relationship before. It's a bizarre thing; I don't recommend it. But as I say, it's not about me. It wasn't that I was lonely. God help me, it wasn't that. I don't want you to think that. I was terrified for Tony. It's just crazy and unnatural for Tony not to be able to talk to his father, and then not to be able to talk to me about the fact that this is not a normal situation, this is not right or correct or good or healthy that he is here to see his father and his father won't talk to him. So you can tell me I did a bad thing but I simply won't accept it.

I wanted to talk to Tony, that's all, as it was an insane situation — that we should be plunged into silence. Forcefully muted by a crazy man.

So Tony was reading *Madame Bovary* on the couch and he looked so sweet and lonely. And I won't speak again about the way the robe hung on him, because you get the idea. I was fully dressed, it wasn't as if I ran around the house naked or in a slip, I was wearing a house dress I often wear — which is emphatically not a dressing gown — and goes down to the floor, and underneath there are these very smart capri pants. So I was more than fully dressed; I might as well have been wearing armour.

Of course the outfit shows off my figure, but what doesn't? I mean, when would I ever wear anything that doesn't? I was making coffee again. I kept making coffee because I didn't know what else to do in the kitchen, and frankly I'm not the world's greatest cook. I mean, I can take care of the baby but that's about it. It's a wonder any of us get any sleep with all the coffee I make. So I leaned out the kitchen door because I just couldn't stand it anymore, the craziness of us not talking. I said "Tony" and he said "Yes?" and he was so hopeful when he looked up from the book, which he probably wasn't really enjoying that much, and I said, "Do you want to talk?"

And he knew what I meant. He absolutely knew. "Yes, I do," he said.

"No, but I mean" — and I sat down on the couch beside him — "I mean, do you really want to talk? For real? About your father?"

"Yes, I do," he said again, and I could tell that he was ready to tear up.

"It's okay," I said, taking a handkerchief out of my pocket. It was certainly the least I could do. I don't know if that's what precipitated it, but suddenly there was a catch in his throat. I handed it to him.

"Why does he hate me?" he asked.

"He doesn't hate you," I said.

"No. He hates me *so much*."

"He doesn't hate you, Tony. Honestly, he loves you."

"Well, he sure has a weird way of showing it," he said.

"No. Honestly, he treats me the same way."

"That's weird," he said. "Are you two having problems? I thought I heard you guys arguing —"

What was the point of all this lying, anyway? "We try and keep it quiet, but of course you'd hear. Yes, we're having problems *galore*."

"Oh, God." He moved slightly closer to me. "Can I ask you a question?"

"Yes, of course." I wasn't about to halt things at this point; we both obviously needed this talk, desperately.

"Does he ..." He looked down, shyly. "Does he ... hurt you?"

I thought he was referring to emotional hurt, so I said, "Yes, of course. It's very hurtful."

"No. I'm sorry, I mean ..." His extreme shyness resumed. I imagine it was because he didn't want to even think of what his father was capable of. "Does he ... Does he physically ... Does he hit you?"

"Well, yes, he has," I said, and then I found myself tearing up. And this was not an act, let me tell you, I was not capable of acting this. Sure there were times early on in my relationship with Nick when his violence seemed to be a part of our physical lovemaking. But that had ended months ago, and now I was simply afraid that he would hit me, and there was nothing I found as humiliating as being afraid, especially afraid of a man. "I don't want you to think about that." I found a handkerchief in my other pocket so I wouldn't be sodden.

"But how can I *not* think about that?" Tony asked, emphatically, through tears. "If he hits you then it means he hates you, too. He hates both of us. A person can't love you and then hit you. Even I know that! A person can be upset about something but when they start to hit you it's just — I don't understand. Why does he hate both of us so much?"

It really was difficult because I could see he was confronting what for him was the face of evil for the very first time. "He doesn't hate you or me," I said. "He hates himself."

"Why would he hate himself?" Tony asked, and this certainly was a good question.

At this point I didn't know what I should say, but I knew that if I didn't say something convincing then Tony would blame himself, which I didn't want to happen under any circumstances. So I said something I probably shouldn't have said: "I think there are some … unconventional things about your father. There are things that he thinks about and maybe, does …" I was thinking about Anthony Curtis and Farley Granger. Of course, I didn't mention their names.

"Do you mean he's some sort of a … pervert?"

"Oh no, I wouldn't say that …" I didn't want him to think those things about Nick, anything but that. "No, it's just that I think he might not be a good man, in some ways that perhaps only he understands and knows about himself, and I don't" — I was being very careful in case Tony had caught my drift — "I don't think he acts on those things, but he just … he tortures himself over it, I think, and he simply hates himself."

Tony appeared to be gathering his courage to defend me. "When was the last time he hit you?"

This was too much. I shouldn't have told him all this — now I felt like a horrible mother. "Don't worry about me," I said. "I'm fine, I'm a grown up. I'm worried about you."

"I just don't want him to hate me anymore," he said. And then he couldn't hold it in anymore and he broke down crying. His tears were soft and gentle, just as he was — and I refuse to blame myself for what I did next, it was a natural thing, a human thing, even a *motherly* thing to do — I hugged him. I hugged him close to me — no apologies — and he hugged me back, and we stayed like that for a long time. Too long.

He was grabbing onto me for dear life, and it seemed I didn't want to let him go, only because I was afraid he would fall, or be lost. Then, at a certain point, the hug became awkward. It was obvious that if I had let him have his way, he would have tried to hold me forever. I tried to separate us, and he finally wrenched himself apart from me and gave me an imploring look. "Don't leave me, Gloria. Please don't leave me. I can't stand it anymore. I can't stand being alone." And suddenly, without any sign — there was no way for me to fend it off, we were sitting that close — he kissed me on the lips. This was the turning point, or it could have been. No, in actual fact it was. Up until that point this could have been a conversation between a mother and a son. But suddenly it had changed, and looking back on it I don't know why I didn't get up and say "No, Tony, no."

This is the way it would have been in the movies — at least since they instituted the Hays Code — as whatever was going on between us would not have been allowed to be portrayed on the silver screen. If I had moved away from Tony at that moment, I would have been playing the good girl Nick was always trying to get me to play in *In a Lonely Place*. But it's no use crying over spilled milk. I didn't do that, I didn't back away, and I suppose if blame is to be laid on me, it would be for not rejecting him at that moment. But is that what *you* would have done? I want you to think about this situation. He felt so alone, and I felt so alone, and this is very significant — *we were alone for the same reason.*

But I have to tell you that I don't know honestly now what difference it would have made if I had gotten up and walked away, because it all moved ahead so quickly after that. Instead of getting up, I kissed him on the cheek. I said: "No, Tony, no. We mustn't." Certainly that may have been what precipitated it, because that was definitely a line from many movies I had been in, when I was resisting the advances from some dangerous male, only to give in. But I'm not going to blame myself anymore, can't you see? Then we were just on each other and we couldn't stop kissing, and then it all went crazy. He was pressing himself against me, we were almost sliding off the couch, and I began to notice something.

Well, one couldn't not notice it, really. It was demanding to be taken notice of. I looked down at his crotch and sticking out there was the most enormous thing I had ever seen, exposed now, through his underwear, between the folds of his robe. I know you will think me vulgar, and I must admit I am being vulgar mentioning this, but at that moment it seemed more than relevant to the whole situation we had found ourselves in. And by that I mean what was significant about the "largesse" of his equipment — and there it was, demanding my attention, or someone's attention, certainly — was that it was much, much larger than his father's. Much, much. His father was, as I may have mentioned, a quite normal male size; although he was a prodigious lover, his equipment was simply adequate. But

Tony was just, well, prodigious. When I saw it, everything became clear to me.

This question had often occurred to me, about fathers and sons. How do they deal with this? What if the son is remarkably well-endowed — much more so than the father? How does the father handle it? I only wonder because there seems to be so much competitiveness involved between fathers and sons. There always seems to be jealousy — of the son on the part of the father — and it's usually deemed to be because the son's fortunes are on the rise and the fathers' are in decline. But is it more than that? What if the very visible sign of the son's manhood is exponentially larger than his father's? How would that make the older man feel? I had no doubt that Nick had seen his son naked, in fact, I knew that they had played racquetball or something at the studio and Tony had talked about the sauna after. The naked rituals men go through, I had heard that there are dark places where perverts go — darkened saunas — and do their business. (What is it about the dark — dark rooms and perversion?)

They were father and son and they must have seen each other naked. And what was going through Nick's mind when he saw that monster hanging between Tony's legs? Is it possible that other men in the sauna had commented on it? Is it possible that Nick could have felt the guilty pangs of — dare I say it (but you know I will) — attraction to his own son?

Well, it was impossible to ignore this humungous being between Tony's legs. I'm sure it would have been as impossible for Nick — if perhaps for different reasons, ultimately —

than it was for me. When I looked down and I saw it, arching toward me, and I looked at Tony's face, that was so tender — so the opposite of that beast between his legs — I knew what lovemaking with him would be like. It would be heaven, because he wouldn't be — as Nick was — *forced* to pummel me in order to precipitate my pleasure. No, he would *serve me*, with a more than ample supply of his love, bringing relief for both of us, from all the damned-up loneliness we had shared before. He was the lover every woman dreams of — an irresistible animal passion mixed with a tender emotional vulnerability.

And so I did a crazy thing — because there that monster was, straining to touch me as it peaked over his underwear, so tortured in its swelling, so to give it, him, and myself some relief — I grabbed hold of it, and stared into Tony's eyes. He uttered a moan I will never forget. And at that very moment the front door opened, and Nick walked in.

I know I should be happy. I should be ecstatic because I had worked so hard for this victory and finally achieved it (by whatever means). It would be natural to feel some guilt over my actions, but I wasn't actually guilty. I was frightened. But then again, I am always generally frightened. I think I must have been frightened coming out of the womb. For instance, though I am an American, I have never fulfilled my military duties. This should have plagued me (it does not) but as I get older it comes back as a nagging thought. When I was in my twenties the Vietnam War was in full swing. If I had crossed the border into the United States at any time during the late sixties, I would have been drafted; so I chose not to. It didn't seem like a momentous decision at the time, though it created a giant fissure between myself and my grandparents, who lived in New York State. They demanded I see them — and then were traumatized by my decision not to — sending me a letter banishing me from their lives. I never saw them again.

So I never did my "service," whereas so many young men did go, and died, or survived with trauma. And it isn't that I feel guilty about it or that I never did it, it is just that I am, constitutionally, a coward. I can't imagine ever doing violence to another living being. I can't even imagine trying very hard to defend myself — only giving up and running. It's different when I am angry, which I rarely am. I suppose anger is responsible for most of what people call bravery, because when I am truly angry it seems I am blind to fear. It's not that I triumph over it, it's just gone. But that rarely happens. Most of the time I am frightened about something, and if I had served in the military, I would have probably run first from my fellow soldiers and then from the enemy. What good would I have been to anyone? I am simply not made that way. I cringe when someone takes aim to hit me, or even when they make a threatening gesture.

So although I lied to the arts council about my heritage, I wasn't particularly afraid of being found out. It certainly seemed that Pierce Kearney was so traumatized with his own decision to identify as Indigenous that he was unlikely to challenge my identification as Black. But the fear that paralyzes me daily has always had more to do with self-doubt than fear of physical violence. And that self-doubt was, paradoxically, magnified by my victory. In the rare instance that I do win an award or an appointment, I automatically presume I am doomed to failure and live in dread of it. It happened when I finally became a full professor, it happened when I began teaching Shakespeare, and it was happening now that I was certain that the arts councils would reward me with a grant. I presumed that I would now get the grant — but though I was now blessed with good fortune, I would do such a bad job at carrying out the project that it would all be a huge failure and expose me to calumny. (Calumny? I love that antique word, Shakespeare uses it in *Hamlet*: "If thou dost marry, I'll give thee this plague / for thy dowry: be thou as chaste as ice, as pure as / snow, thou shalt not escape calumny. Get thee to a / nunnery, go; farewell.")

But *calumny* means underserved curses; all my curses will be deserved. I will prove to be a terrible producer and a terrible director. I have never been a creative writer, have never written a play, I have only written this — whatever it is, I refuse to dignify it by calling it a diary — which no one will ever read unless — as I have mentioned before — I am either dead or in jail. I composed the academic papers required for my career goals, but they are of little consequence. And then there are my "people skills," if they can even be called that. I am generally frightened of people, and afraid specifically of angering or upsetting them; I want too much to be liked. But this is all in vain. Who would ever like me? Especially now that I am physically repellent and so obviously gay in a way that reminds people of things they would rather forget.

Yes, I do occasionally make friends with sympathetic females; but *Venus and Adonis: The Play* — as I am now calling it — is to be cast with only young men. Young men of whom I am eternally petrified because I am eternally attracted to them. Perhaps I will hire a young performer who is an ex-student of mine and I will be perilously attracted to him; I will act out. There will be a scandal, I will be ejected from Canadian Actor's Equity (I was made a member many years ago in order to act in an Equity play) but then again, one can't be ejected, it is a union — unions are like flies on shit, you can never get rid of them — so I will be a disgraced member for life. My name will be in the papers ("University Prof Hired Ex-Students — Lusted After Them"). It will be lust alone that is the crime and I will be guiltier than sin. Does this sound like a ridiculous fantasy?

But my fantasy is completely self-fulfilling because my eternal self-doubt paralyzes me. With every two steps forward I make ten steps back. Every achievement only emphasizes my inadequacy. I cannot move ahead as other people do; I can only operate in reverse. I am a doodlebug. Doodlebugs walk backwards; they leave a messy trail behind them. That is me. My victory will always only affirm my failure as an artist, as a professor, and, most importantly, as a person. I am paralyzed with fear, but that is nothing new. What then, should I do?

It was quick again, after that. I don't remember because the moment was so filled with Nick's rage and our fear; I have never been as afraid as that before. I hope I will never be again, but now I am just living in fear and I can't get out. It is a nightmare, my worst nightmare, and I will tell you why, but first I have to tell you what happened. It's all a blur, but Nick hurled himself at us, and they began to fight, and I tried to separate them. And all the time he was punching his son he was hurling insults at me, calling me a slut, et cetera, there's no point in repeating it; it's the kind of thing he had been calling me for months, nay, years. Now I realize, you know, *that* is the thing to be afraid of in men. They look at you in a way sometimes — I used to think it was a lustful look, now I know that what makes it so compelling is that it is a look of both lust and hate; the two emotions seem to co-exist. I swear, after seeing that look in Nick's eyes that day, I will never trust that look if I see it in a man's eyes again. In the future it must be lust only; no hate. Then I realized that Nick would kill both of us if this went on, and I grabbed Tony's arm. I pulled him away, out the front door, and we ran out of the house. Nick came out yelling. But his sense of propriety would not take him beyond that. He ran back inside the house again, and Tony and I stood on the front lawn; thank heavens Nick's old robe had a belt, which Tony had pulled tight around him.

Then we heard a most paralyzing noise. It was the sound of Nick destroying the inside of the house. We could hear him roaring — it was the roar of a lion, and then there was the sound of him pounding on the walls and breaking things. It seemed that he was pulling down the bookshelves. When we heard him pull over the upright piano in the den with a primeval roar it was too much for me. I grabbed Tony's arm and I told him to stay with my mother for the night (she had been taking care of Timmy while Tony stayed with us). He gestured to his robe, but I said she just lives two blocks way, so he was gone at a run. God knows what the neighbours would think, but since the neighbours were all Hollywood stars with their own marital scandals percolating at top speed, probably no one would notice. Then I marched out and walked around the block (we have big blocks in Hollywood, thank God). I stayed away for a long time. About a half an hour later I made my way through the gate, but I could still hear the sounds of destruction. I walked directly back out again and stayed out for the afternoon, pondering things in a park.

In a weird way, I think I was calmed by this expression of Nick's anger. I fantasized that he was getting his rage out of his system. Looking back on it now, I see that would have been impossible; Nick was always in a rage, and he was then, and is now, fundamentally crazy. So how crazy was I, to imagine that merely wrecking the house would appease him?

When I finally went back inside there didn't seem to be anyone there. I locked the door to our bedroom (it's something I insisted on when I discovered how drunk Nick would get night after night — then I would lock him out and he slept on the couch). I hibernated in the bedroom until it was time to sleep. When I woke up the next day there was not a sound in the house. I was not required at the studio that day, so I decided to go to my mother's. When I got there, Tony was having breakfast with my mother and sister (she had found him some suitable male clothing that was a little big on his lithe frame); it seemed an idyllic family scene. I told Tony he would have to go back to the house. As far as I could imagine, Nick would not be there. He would not miss a day of work at the studio, especially for a domestic quarrel; that was certain. I told Tony, in private, to lock his bedroom door from the inside if he heard Nick come in the front door. Perhaps I should have talked with him, but it just didn't seem to me that Tony and I should be together at that time; not only did I not know what to say to him, but I was confused about my feelings. It all seemed wrong. I'm sorry now that I did that, it was a huge mistake to let Tony go back to the house. If I hadn't done that, I wouldn't be in the state I am in now. I wouldn't be living in perpetual fear.

I am not a human being who can deal with fear. Do you understand me? I am not meant to be afraid. It is because I think a woman like me is vulnerable to every kind of attack, I see that now, after this fiendish mess of a relationship, that being beautiful and owning your desire is the worst combination in a woman, and that you will always be punished for it. Being beautiful means being physically weak; it is part of how a woman's beauty is defined, but when we dare to desire we are punished by the men who are afraid of our desire, and because we are physically weak, they are capable of killing us.

It's a wonder Nick didn't kill me. But after what he said to me when I saw him the next day — well, now he has me terrified to death.

So the day after the incident he was away all day at work. Tony stayed in his room. I didn't see him. And I haven't even told you about the house. It was as if a bomb had exploded. You couldn't have lived there, in the living room or the kitchen or the den. He wrecked the coffeemaker, but early in the evening I managed to find a kettle and put it on the burner to make myself some coffee. I heard the front door open and my first instinct was to run, but then I knew I would be leaving Tony alone in this bombsite of a house with a man who hated him certainly as much as he hated me. The other thing you have to know was that at this point I wasn't the creature of fear that I have now become. I thought I could do what I used to do; which was to brave it out. I opened the kitchen door and Nick had turned a chair upright so he could sit in it.

He sat silently, looking at me. We stared each other down for a long time. Then I went back into the kitchen because the kettle was whistling. He said, "Where do you think you're going?"

I said, defiantly, "I don't want to burn down the house." At that strange moment, it was as if everything might have gone back to what it was before. That was the crazy thing with Mr. Nicholas Ray. We had fought so violently so many times and said so many horrible things to each other, and no matter what you say, that can cause a strange bond between a couple. Yes it can. When you go to the limit, sexually and in terms of the violence — the volatility of your emotions — when you go beyond saying what you thought you ever might say, when you stare someone down and scream "I hate you like I've never hated anyone before!" and then find yourself kissing the same man the next day, it creates a glue that is stickier than any old marriage vow. So for that moment it felt as if — yes, I know it's crazy — but it felt like we might go back to same old, same old. But no. I took the kettle off and took the time to completely pour myself a coffee, cream, sugar, and all, and re-entered what was left of the living room. He was sitting in exactly the same way as he was sitting before I had gone back in the kitchen. In fact, he was motionless, as if he hadn't moved at all for the last couple of minutes; he was like a statue or a zombie.

Then he spoke: "I've made a recording."

It was like he had stabbed me in the heart. I knew exactly what he was talking about. Nick was obsessed with tape recordings. The possible applications of this new technology fascinated him; he had actually put a "wire" on himself for several meetings at the studio, because he's always been paranoid, though he hadn't had the courage to use it on anyone. Would he have the courage to use this? I played dumb. "What are you saying?" I asked. But he knew he had me. He was a demon sitting in that chair.

"I took the liberty of sitting down with my son and asking him a few questions."

"You didn't!" I was spitting out my fury. "How could you? How could you —"

"Well, Gloria —"

"How could you bring him into this?" I asked.

"How could I bring him into this? Oh, Gloria, that's a little like the pot calling the kettle black." He fancied himself some sort of grand inquisitor.

"You know what I mean," I said. "Leave Tony alone. You've done enough damage."

"I've done Tony damage? *I've* done damage?" He sighed. It seemed that was all that was left of his rage. This frightened me more than anything. "No, Gloria, it is you who has damaged my son. And I have it all down on tape. He told me the whole story of the seduction."

"There was no seduction." I spit out the word *seduction*; it was pornographic and completely inappropriate.

"That's not what Tony says."

"He couldn't have said that, because it's not true."

"Well, he did say that, and I'm sorry to say, Gloria, but the police aren't going to look very kindly on this. It's a clear case of an adult molesting a minor, and, much worse, a step-mother molesting her son." He clucked at me. He actually clucked. Nick knew that Tony was not actually my son, but I didn't bother to correct him. "No, this won't look very good on the record at all. I'm afraid your career is over, Gloria."

"You wouldn't do that. You wouldn't dare do that," I hissed at him. "It would ruin your career as well as mine. Nobody would be able to talk about anything but the scandal. Nobody would come near you. And what about our movie?"

"*Our* movie? *OUR* movie?" He clucked again. "Suddenly it's *our* movie. Well, I don't know about you, Gloria, but I don't give a fuck about *our* movie. I only care about my son."

I couldn't believe — or rather, I could — him saying this now, as if he had cared anything about his son before, when he hadn't done anything but hurt him, ignore him, threaten him, make him feel small. But his son wasn't small, was he? And his father knew it, and maybe that was the problem. No. I couldn't believe it. It wasn't true. Tony couldn't possibility have said that I molested him and there was no way Nick had the guts to go public with these vile lies. No way. But somewhere, deep inside, I wasn't completely sure that was true. I got up, went to the bedroom, packed my things, and left the house. I went to stay with my mother. I didn't say another word to him and haven't since then. Now I live in terror.

* * * * * *

(I intend to attach this to the beginning of the play. It seems to me that a small young man — someone who looks barely nineteen years old — should read it, while wearing wings like cupid. But otherwise, he should be naked.)

In Defence of Venus
Venus and Adonis, *by Mr. William Shakespeare, has been sadly and unjustly ignored. Critics rarely deal with it; yet it was a "bestseller" in its time. One of the reasons for that may be because the poem is somewhat pornographic. Pornography did exist in 1590, when* Venus and Adonis *was first distributed, and that pornography was much more explicit. (One thinks, for instance, of Thomas Nashe's justly famous poem about an encounter in a brothel with a sex toy — often referred to as "Nashe's Dildoe.") What is there about* Venus and Adonis *that would cause Elizabethans to adore it and cause us to ignore it?*

I charge that the cause lies in the agency given to one woman. Venus, in the poem, is older, and she chases after a young man in the woods. The young man is a teenager, clearly, and the woman is just past her prime. It's pathetic that she is a goddess chasing after a mortal, because she cannot seduce him without persuading him. But he will not be persuaded. He is, in effect, raped. It's important to note that the boy is described in lush and delicious detail just as would be a female virgin of the period. He has cheeks that are both white and red; damask is most often the word associated with English beauty. One sees it occasionally in a youth today — whether they be male or female. There is a flush on the cheeks, but the skin is very pale, so the contrast provides extra visual pleasure. There is also the lascivious detail that a cheek almost always becomes flushed as someone becomes sexually aroused, and is a sure sign of orgasm. So a description of a young cheek that is pale and rose seems to express nothing less than the dawn of desire.

Venus extemporizes at length about the beauty of the boy and uses all of her womanly powers of persuasion, yet he must hunt his boar. He does not kill the boar, the boar kills him; the boy is gored in the thigh. This goring is a metaphorical screwing; so to speak. It is not even metaphorical; the boy is penetrated in the thighs as a result of his encounter with a goddess.

After this, Venus — to mourn him — curses all love. Her curse is one of the most perfect poetic passages in all of western literature. Venus's curse in Venus and Adonis *is meant to explain why love will be forever futile:*

> *[Love] shall be sparing and too full of riot,*
> *Teaching decrepit age to tread the measures;*
> *The staring ruffian shall it keep in quiet,*
> *Pluck down the rich, enrich the poor with treasures;*
> *It shall be raging-mad and silly-mild,*
> *Make the young old, the old become a child.*

Her heartbreak is gorgeous and ironic. We identify with her rage and pain, and we understand, paradoxically, the reason she might have decided to make love so difficult for us all, in revenge for the death of her one true love.

Do the implications of all this need to be explained? Just in case they do; our enjoyment of the fantasy requires that we sympathize with Venus; it is impossible to love the poem without thinking that her lust is somehow justifiable.

Is it? Here, perhaps, we come to the key question. Is any lust justifiable? It is ultimately an unanswerable question; lust cannot be justified; it simply is or is not. Lust is a fact of life — like a hurricane or a waterfall. We can lead an expedition into the eye of a hurricane; however, it is mostly likely to devour us. But we can't ask, "Whither, hurricane? Why?"

Nevertheless, it is clear from many modern interpretations of Shakespeare's poem that Venus's lust is so unpalatable to the modern reader that critics must obliterate it. The disgust is formidable. Critics say things such as "No one can sympathize with Venus's somewhat selfish, heartless nature."

How do I tell you this ...? All lust is heartless and selfish, that's what makes lust so exciting. Men have been able to get away with nursing their own heartless, selfish lust for years, without being criticized, except by moralists. Immoral desire has even been ennobled by the tragic operatic figure of Don Juan — so why shouldn't Venus be allowed hers? Perhaps we should ask this question: What kind of a world would we be living in if women were allowed the same parameters and licence for their lust as that given to men? What if the world was built around women's lust instead of men's? Perhaps Elizabethans were able to sympathize with Venus because of their queen, precisely because their head of state was a woman who had confessed in one of her most famous speeches to being of an essentially ambivalent gender. (Elizabeth is purported to have said: "Tho born a woman, I have the heart of a man.") Venus is the standard bearer for a sexualized matriarchy, a matriarchy not based on the fecundity but on the brutal power of woman's lust.

Make no doubt about it, women's lust leaves the man squirming, gored, and raped. And why shouldn't he be raped, as women have been raped for centuries? Is it simply the matter of an eye for an eye? No, it is the just acknowledgement of male beauty, of the tender concupiscence of a flaccid penis resting against the vulnerable swing of testicles that graze so gently a muscular thigh. For what is the beauty of the male but an endless, mysterious potential? We speak of a woman as being a mystery; her poetics are that of an undiscovered country. But no, it is the man who is mysterious — for at any moment that penis might become erect. Look! It is rising! And do we really know why? Isn't that the glory? And is that not more than an undiscovered country, is that not an undiscovered universe? For there is nothing quite so beautiful as a question for which there is no answer.

I knew it would not be good for Tony, but I couldn't stand the suspense. I wrestled with it for a long time. Tony should be done with all this, he shouldn't have to think of this incident again, but then — I thought — his father would not let him forget it. I couldn't imagine they would talk about it after the damned recording, that recording would be tough enough, but they would live in the shadow of it, the two of them, in that wreck of a house. I knew what it would be; an oppressive silence. Tony, having done his father's bidding after making that blasted recording, would expect his father to repay him with his love; but Nick would not give a morsel, not even a scrap, of affection; he was very good at that. Tony would gaze at his father with those gentle doe-like eyes to no avail. So every day Tony would be re-living the scene over and over again, and experiencing the pain of this renewed unbearable distance between him and his father. If I was to ask him about that insane tape recording was it going to victimize him any further? No. And I couldn't stand it any longer. I had to know.

Nick had changed the telephone number but I managed to get it. I explained to the assistant director at the studio that Nick had gone quite insane and I feared for Tony's safety living alone with his father in that house. The A.D. was easily persuaded; they had all had enough of Nick at this point. The studio's attitude was that if *In a Lonely Place* didn't make any money then they would have no reason to have anything to do with Nicholas Ray ever again.

So I had the phone number, and I waited for a day when Nick was most certainly at the studio (thank God I didn't have to see him, ever, all of my scenes were in the can), and I called. At first Tony didn't answer. I let the phone ring and ring. He knew who it was. I felt awful; I knew why he didn't want to answer, he knew what I was going to ask him. Every ring was torture, and then he finally picked up the phone. Tony immediately apologized, tearing up. "I'm sorry, Gloria," he said. He had never ever called me mother. I thought of this suddenly. Nick had tried his best to get Tony to call me Mother, but it just never stuck; he insisted on calling me Gloria from the start. This was a bee in Nick's bonnet, a bee that wouldn't go away, it was a frustrating, inscrutable "bee" — as bees can sometimes be. But it should have made him understand from the start that the ridiculous fantasy that this teenaged boy might be in any way thought of or conceived to be my son was an unbelievable, unacceptable fiction of staggering proportions.

I said, "What do you have to be sorry for? Don't be sorry."

He started to cry. "For the ... for the tape." There he said it. Suddenly, the tape recording was a reality; I had been hoping against hope that it was just a threat, that Nick had made it all up to punish me, but most of all as a control tactic, because he knew very well that the threat of it was enough to put the fear of God in me. But now I knew there was actually a tape. It existed. It was somewhere, someone could hear it. In fact, the police might be listening to it right now.

"Listen, I don't blame you. I would never blame you. You're just a pawn in all this. Nothing is your fault. It's your father's fault, and it isn't that he doesn't love you, it's that for some reason he needs to withhold that love from you, and torture you. He's done the same thing to me. As soon as someone loves him he takes his affection away, he makes himself unavailable. It's torture, it's manipulation, it's not your fault. So that's the first thing I want you to understand. When do you go back to school?"

"Tomorrow," he said, choking on the word. Thank God I had found him. It might have been very difficult, even embarrassing, to contact him at military school.

"Well, at least you'll be done with him, Tony, for a while."

"Will you come visit me at school, Gloria?"

This was an insane and impossible idea. I said, "I don't know if I can."

"Please, please come. I'll die without you."

"Don't say that. Please don't say it. If anything, you have to keep yourself alive for me. If you can't do it for your father, do it for me." Of course, I shouldn't have said that, but it was an understandable impulse; he was, in effect, threatening suicide.

"So is there a possibility we might be able to be together?"

Oh, God. What could I say? "Who knows what will happen in the future, Tony."

"'Who knows' — do you really mean that?"

"Of course, I do. No one can predict the future."

"So we might be together?"

I spoke very carefully. "I said ... anything might happen. That's what the future is."

"Oh, God, you've given me a reason to live." This was a very fourteen-year-old thing to say, but I was nevertheless somewhat calmed by the fact that I had figured out a way to stall his suicidal impulses.

Now I felt I could ask him. "Tony, I — do you mind — I hate asking you this, but he's threatening to go public with this tape recording."

"I know," said Tony.

"You mean, you think he might?"

"He says he will," said Tony, "but I … I don't know."

"You think he might not, then?" I was desperate for any clue to what Nick might do.

"He hasn't done anything yet." Well, that was a blessing, anyway. I had to treat this whole situation like a death sentence — I would have to take one day at a time and find hope when I could.

"As I say, I just hate asking you this, but it's driving me crazy. Can you tell me what he asked you on that tape?"

"It was horrible," said Tony. "He tied me up."

"He tied you up?"

"And then he said he would punch me out."

"You must have been terrified."

"I was. I was at his mercy. And then he pulled out the tape recorder and said that if I didn't answer the questions to his satisfaction that he would beat me to a pulp."

"Oh my God, Tony." As horrible it was to hear all this, it was a somewhat of a relief. I suddenly wished I was tape recording *this* telephone conversation. It would certainly be useful in court. Whatever Tony had said on that tape, it was not voluntary, and certainly not uncoerced. "So what did he ask you?'"

"He asked me how it happened."

"And what did you say?"

"I told him."

"What did you tell him?"

"I told him that we got into a conversation about him, and about how bad I felt about our relationship, and that you and me, we hugged each other for a long time —"

"You said that we hugged each other, not that I hugged you?"

"Well that's what happened."

"Yes, that is what happened, Tony."

"And then I told him that I kissed you, and that you told me not to do that."

"You said that? You told him that?"

"Well, of course. It happened."

"So what else did you say?"

"I said that, well — then I told him that he came in after that."

"Is that all you said, Tony?"

"That's absolutely all I said."

"Well" — I was afraid to hope — "that doesn't sound so bad. I mean, it's horrible that you had to go through all that with him, but it doesn't sound like there's much on the tape that incriminates me. I mean I'm sure you can understand how worried I am."

"Well, that's the strange thing," he said. This sent a chill down my spine.

"What do you mean?"

"I mean, I said just what I just told you, and that's the story, that's the real story of what happened. It's the truth and I was surprised after that big buildup and him threatening me and everything, but he just said, 'That's all I need,' and then he untied me. And I couldn't believe it. I asked him, 'That's all you want to know?' Because I knew what he was doing, I knew he was trying to make you look bad, and I just couldn't see anything in what I said that would make you look bad, but he just said — like, as if what I said was such a big deal — he said, 'I think I have everything I need to know, and everything the police need to know.' I don't get it. I just don't get it. I mean, nothing really bad happened. He came in before something bad could happen."

This was, of course, wishful thinking on Tony's part. Nick had seen me grabbing Tony and, obviously, the whole scene could be viewed as very incriminating to me. Then it suddenly occurred to me that Nick had lost his nerve. When it came down to it, he couldn't bear to ask Tony, to talk about that moment, that moment when we briefly rolled around and I had touched his son. It was Nick who was afraid of this, of having Tony repeat the details out loud. If he was that afraid of what he saw, then he might be afraid to take all this to court. Or, on the other hand, he might also believe — and he might be right — that even the way Nick described it on that tape, it still incriminated me, because I was, after all, more than fifteen years Tony's senior and technically his stepmother. This was what I wouldn't be able to get out of my mind.

"Are you all right, Gloria?"

"Yes. I'm as all right as I can be."

"Will you think about visiting me at school?"

"I'll certainly think about it," I said.

"Can I write you letters?"

"Yes. Yes, write me," I said. "You can send them to my mother's."

"Okay, I will. And one last thing before you go away."

"Yes?"

"I love you, Gloria."

"Yes, Tony, I love you, too," I tried to say in a way that was not motherly, or passionate, but just kind. And then I put down the phone.

What next? I wasn't entirely sure, since my heart was set on failure. But the only way to achieve that failure (if one can speak of such a paradoxical thing) would be to move forward. I placed an ad for an audition online. I said that we had received funding — this was my own way of courting doom, because certainly to assume something like that was a false braggadocio that would be punished in the twinkling of an eye. The ad was circumspect, modest, unprepossessing. "Professor Denton Moulton is looking for young male actors (aged 18–25) to star in his production of *Venus and Adonis: The Play*. The funding is secured, the pay is TBA. If you would like to audition, please email a resume to —" and then I left my school email address.

For a while nothing happened. And then the responses began to come in. Are all young male actors between the ages of eighteen and twenty-five beautiful? I expect so — or perhaps all young men of that age are beautiful to me now. I have noticed that the age of the men that attract me has become younger, year by year. It's quite frightening. I daren't speculate on the outcome, though I've never fostered any sexual feelings for children. But there was a time when any old thirty-year-old was young enough to suit my fancy. Now it seems that my fantasy age is closer to twenty-one. Everything seems to be spiralling toward something; it's not pretty and probably prophetic. One of the resumes I received was from a young man who is perhaps twenty-three, his name is Lyon Jones — he is an ex-student of mine, and his is an unlikely name for a real person. He is real though. Very real, as I soon found out.

I should explain that some of the young men who responded to my ad were, necessarily I think, ex-students of mine. I say *necessarily* because there is really no other reason that anyone might decide to answer such an ad. The title of the play is strange enough, and I have no credentials — that is, to anyone but my ex-students. It's the inevitable result of being a professor. One engenders a certain respect. It's the nature of the job, really. I have seen, at the university, various bumbling fools and various nefarious characters who nevertheless succeeded in gaining the devotion of their students. One can't overexaggerate the power of an institution — and of a position — to awaken adoration in the eyes of the young.

They really are starry-eyed in some respects, and though many will automatically make fun of you and treat you with disrespect, even that comes from a place that is, in its own perverse way, intimidated by your power. Even if they want to pull you down, it is because they think you are so high up.

I had a student last year who I saw convicted of plagiarism. (Unfortunately, the punishment is now so lax, I wonder why I bother.) Her mistake was using the word *quotidian* in an essay, which, in case you don't know, is an antique synonym for *daily* and a word no one would use in a normal conversation, and certainly not in an undergraduate paper, unless they were not in their right mind. Noticing the word, I googled some of her other sentences; they were clearly passages from SparkNotes. The girl wasn't the least bit repentant, claimed that she had misunderstood the assignment. (The assignment was more than clear. All my assignments are.) When it was over she didn't as much apologize as try and reinstate herself in my affections, which was impossible. I couldn't fathom her motives, as she seemed too smart to make this mistake. But then I remembered back to the first class, when I had made a scheduling error in my first version of the outline. I remembered that she corrected me, she and her friend Lindy (her name was Lucy; they were Lucy and Lindy, and they always sat together). I had been thankful for the help, as I had misscheduled the dates, and when I brought the new outline to class Lucy and Lindy were laughing visibly. (They were both large, rather unattractive girls, with long brown hair that obscured their features, which was probably a good idea.)

Obviously they thought they had caught me in a stupid mistake, and they had. But it was the glee with which they took up what they obviously conceived of as their victory over a dumb, pretentious senile old hack — which I'm sure is what they thought me to be — that made me realize, when I discovered her plagiarism, that Lucy had most likely thought me ridiculous from the beginning, and this was the reason for her crime.

But this kind of skepticism of the powers that be is rare these days; and the closest thing, sadly, that there is to revolution. Unlike in the sixties, when I was at community college (I took an acting course back then, when I wanted to be an actor) and there were always rumours of rebellion, strike, and even violence in response to what was considered the tyranny of the university bureaucracy. Today most students do what they are told quite blindly; it's almost frightening. And the respect they have for me is disturbing, too, because I know it is so undeserved.

So it would make sense that ex-students from my class would be the only ones to respond to my ad. And seeing those names and those photos of those beautiful boys who answered my audition call, all of whom I had given myself permission to desire (they were *ex*-students and unlikely to become future ones), made for me a sudden swelling expectation of what I perceived to be my inevitable downfall. It was almost certain that I would behave badly under the circumstances; molest some poor unsuspecting beauty — in a passive way probably. I would stare too long, or invite them to my sad, old apartment for a late-night dinner, or merely graze their "whatever," and pretend it was an accident, far too many times.

Well, little did I know that the matter would be taken out of my hands. Now I must admit that before I go to the back room of my favourite bar to seek favours from those who lurk in the dark, I have exactly three drinks at a neighbouring bar that has no back room. This is a bar where young men — some young and some even younger — do hang out, and I stick out like a sore thumb for no one there is quite as ancient as I. I stay there for about an hour. The youngsters view me with fear and circle far from me when they pass so as not to be thought flirtatious. What is the origin of the shunning? I think it is not so much because they are afraid I will molest them — I am unprepossessing to the extreme. What they fear instead is that I am a harbinger of things to come; a portent of what constitutes their inevitable and depressing end. They know somehow in their frisky, cocky, randy little souls that they will, if they are lucky (the only other choice is early death), someday end up like me — a dark, slightly bent, repellant figure, frequenting bars that he has absolutely no business being at, and absolutely no chance of being picked up in. All of these youngsters have dreams of true gay love and marriage, but many I'm sure have witnessed divorces on the part of their own parents, or sense how essentially fragile the promise of marriage between two randy young men might be. Thus, they avoid me, literally like the plague. That is, *usually*.

Now, getting back to Lyon Jones; he was one of the first young men to answer the audition call. When he was in my class eight years ago he was a very memorable boy. He was only seventeen years old; now he would be a ripe old twenty-five. What I remember most about him were his thighs. Of course, he never displayed them to me naked, but I did notice them because he wore those skinny jeans that so many students wear these days; and his rear and legs were just massive, in just the right way. From the tightness around his crotch it appeared that something else might be massive, too. I was quite hypnotized by the hefty presence of his lower body. He had a very large head — leonine, need it be said — with a mass of straight black hair always falling rakishly to his eyebrow. He also seemed to be fundamentally stupid, which simply added to his allure.

I hadn't thought about him for many years, but when he sent in his picture in response to my online ad for actors, I recognized him immediately and he set my old heart a-beating. I was at the bar that I frequent before going to the back room, on the third of my three drinks — so I was starting to get a little bit sexually excited and was effectively loosening my inhibitions, which was the purpose of the drinks in the first place, and suddenly Lyon appeared. I was standing at the bottom of a stairway with my back to it, and I could hear someone behind me saying my name: "Denton. Dr. Denton Moulton." He repeated this a couple of times and I didn't dare look back. Then he staggered down the stairs and stood in front of me. I recognized him, and he was somewhat older, obviously, than when I knew him at seventeen but no less gorgeous, wearing a rather fetching trench coat and swaying with drink. He stood directly in front of me, stared at me for a second or two. Then he leaned forward and kissed me. It was alarming and very exciting. Then he stood back. "The brilliant Dr. Denton Moulton. You're fucking brilliant," he said. "You know that. You know how brilliant you are? World renowned, eh?"

It's true we are actually *expected* to be world renowned at the university, and it is something that we put on our web-pages, all of us professors, whether we are actually world re-nowned or not. Then he started to kiss me again, and as sexy as he was it began to hurt somewhat. It actually hurt my lips. I pushed him away gently, not because the kiss was unwanted (I was in as much of a state of arousal as a man my age might be) but because I began to wonder about his motives and his actual ability — in his full inebriated state — to kiss *anyone*.

He pulled back, seeming to realize how drunk he was. He slurred his words. "What's the matter, Dr. Moulton? Am I not good enough? Am I not good enough for you? Am I not good enough for your fucking play?" Then he raised a hand as if to slap me. I raised my hand to protect myself, and then he came in for another kiss instead. This time it really hurt my lips, but he had opened his coat and was pressing the full weight of his powerful lower body against mine, and this was very arousing indeed. Then he looked at me and said, "You don't like me. You don't respect me. I'm not good enough for you and your fucking play. How could you? How *could* you?"

I had no idea now what he was talking about. It occurred to me that possibly he had emailed me in reply to my ad but I hadn't responded. Then I remembered that I had, in fact, delayed my response because I didn't know if I could handle having him in my play. I was, after all, so desperately attracted to him — so it was quite possible I hadn't responded at all. Obviously, his present actions indicated this had been the case.

"I'm sorry ..." I said softly.

"No, you don't want me ..." he said and staggered back. He started up the stairs behind me again saying, "Just a minute, I'll be right back." And it occurred to me that he was going to bring a posse of n'er-do-wells, of renegade youngsters, to beat me up and/or kill me. But standing there, waiting for him, I desperately wanted him to come back. I found I was nurturing a generous amount of expectation without even having to muster an erection — it was just there. I was actually overflowing with emotion and yearning.

Then the assistant manager of the bar came up to me. I've been going to the bar for years, he knows me. He had obviously been watching the whole sordid scene. "Was that guy bothering you, Dr. Moulton?" He was very protective — because, like so many, he was impressed by the "Dr." attached to my name.

I didn't know what to say. I was, of course, bothered by Lyon Jones, but part of it involved a way that I had not been bothered in years, and was thus quite welcome. "Well, that is —" I couldn't finish my sentence.

He looked at me sympathetically. "Would you like me to get rid of him? He's pretty drunk." I felt bad about having Lyon Jones thrown out. But this kind man was now making it quite clear that I should *not* be kissing this boy — in his own tactful way — and that I was perhaps participating in what might prove to be an embarrassing public incident. At which point Lyon appeared as if on cue, made his way down the stairs again, and stood, swaying, in front of me. The manager, who was quite a sturdy fellow, placed his hands on Lyon, intending to drag him out of the bar.

Lyon pleaded with me. "Dr. Moulton, you're not actually doing this to me, are you? No ... you're not doing this. I can't believe you would —" and he was gone. It was gratifying, I suppose, to have my honour so protected by the powers that be. But dear me, I shouldn't cast this crazy boy in my play, should I? Or were they all crazy? Isn't that what being that age is all about?

There were no letters for a while. And for a while I thought Tony had forgotten me. But I knew that it was not possible we would ever forget each other. And it might be useful for you to think — or you might actually believe — that we should both be psychoanalyzed. I know about psychoanalysis, it's quite popular, people always talk about it. I've never set much store by it.

After all, what would be gained of a psychoanalytical view of the situation? I have read my Shakespeare. The situation might be thought Oedipal; you probably think it was. Tony was the young Hamlet, and I the incestuous, fiendish Gertrude. (At least this analysis equates Nick with Claudius!) But what is the use of it all? Was Tony looking for a mother figure? Undoubtedly he was. Was I looking for a son figure? Can't you see how fruitless this all is? And it all just seems to point to a big fat "so what?" So what if we are neurotic and expressing unhealthy needs. I've never known a love that is healthy. How is it ever to be healthy, since we learn about love from our parents, and even if they are dear — as my mother and father were to me — there was most likely something wrong with them, something about them, about their relationship with me, that I misunderstood, or that caused me pain.

I'm sorry. I just can't go on with this. I am not saying that Tony and I are destined to be together. I will say though, that fifteen years isn't quite as large an age gap as one might imagine. It is technically a generation; but just barely. There's nothing *Romeo and Juliet* about what happened to us, and that is why I think it might have legs in its own strange way. I'm not saying that we will end up with each other. I'm saying that we will always love each other. We shared something — and not what you think, but *instead* a kind of bond and intimacy between two people that will never go away. We both experienced the same pain, for the same reason, at exactly the same time — and we reached out to each other. And, really, you can moralize about that if you really want to.

Okay, go ahead, psychoanalyze it all you want, but that's just *inhuman* of you, don't you see? We had a connection; we needed each other terribly for that one moment, and we came together and touched each other quite literally, and I won't have you sully that. And is your life so perfect? And what is "perfect"? Don't we just muddle along, all of us, married or unmarried, lonely and/or alone? But if we're still *alive* inside we just want to find a real connection with another human being. And that's why anything happens; because people *must connect*. The tragic irony is what that means (for some) is lashing out at another person or even doing them permanent harm — which explains, I think, the way Nick treated me. And that's why I can't blame him, because ultimately, he was human, too. But when connecting is as tender as what happened between Tony and I —

Well. I just can't stand you judging it. And I won't have you judging it. So there.

Anyway. What happened after Tony went off to military school was not very pleasant, as you might well imagine. I found myself suddenly afraid — not of just Nick's threats about releasing the tape recording but of everything. It was bizarre; so very unlike me; I had lost control.

In order to regain some control, I started to institute divorce proceedings. I cited emotional cruelty. I never went near the physical cruelty part, even though I could very well have. The purpose of this was to test Nick, because it seemed to me that he, like me, just wanted to be rid of this whole affair without scandal. I was right. At least, he hasn't contested the accusations, because all I claimed in my case was that he ignored me and that made it impossible for me to work.

This was the truth — as the kind of treatment I endured with him did involve being ignored, emotionally. And I couldn't work with such a madman. And, of course, he had ignored Tony and that was a very special crime in a father. I had to wait for several months for the actual appearance in court, which I knew would be a circus. And I must say I was behaving very badly in my — what shall we call it — my personal life. Oh, yes, I have Timmy and I always will have Timmy, I don't mean *that* personal life (as long as Nick doesn't try and get custody of Timmy ever — that is, try and take him away from me, but so far so good, and I can't start worrying about that now). There's nothing terribly personal about being a mother. And Nick will get visitation, I'm not a monster. No. I'm talking about my fear of virtually everything — which means that I was not capable, in my own mind at least, of being alone. The only way I could not feel so desperately alone was that I *somehow* arranged to be with a man every night. (I suppose I could have hired a nurse!)

There were some recurring nights with recurring gentlemen — actors, production designers, that sort of thing, and oh, yes, of course "best boys." (I've always been fond of that particular cinematic terminology — best boys go running about aiming the lights at us actors, don't you know?!) Not every encounter resulted in something happening in the bedroom, but to tell you the honest truth it was such a relief when they slept beside me. That's all I really wanted.

And some of them agreed to do that. It was very sweet. Some did not entirely understand, but tried to. One lovely man — when he was unable to run to my bedside — sent me a Western Union Telegram delivery, and I persuaded the young man who delivered the telegram to stay in my room for some time. I won't go into the details (which aren't really that racy) but the young man was kind enough to keep me company for a while.

And I'm not kidding about this, though it may sound ludicrous to you, I was literally terrified that someone might come in through the window. Not Nick, but someone like Nick, or the spirit of Nick — or my own guilt. I don't know. I was acting incredibly crazily.

Then, when the trial did come, it was the oddest day. I was terrified because I decided at the last minute to testify that Nick hit me, which I knew would complicate things and make Nick angry, but it was the truth, and I knew it would ensure that I would get the divorce, and, anyway, what was Nick going to do? Start going on about Tony and I at the proceedings? I knew that I had to look fabulous and in this case it was completely practical matter because it would distract everyone. And I really hoped that all the headlines would be about the dress.

I had Lana Turner in the back of my mind, because *Postman* had been such a hit and had started a craze when she dressed in all white to go swimming. On the one hand, I knew it was dangerous to reference the "femme fatale" image, but after all I *was* one and would be one forever in the public's eyes, if there is such a nebulous thing as the "eye of the public."

Ultimately, I chose a white hat and sweater and shoes — there is nothing quite like white shoes — I think it is the sheer impracticality of them that is so eternally daring — and, of course, white jewellery. The dress was jet black. The white hat was a beret, by the way, and I wore my hair in a pageboy. I also wore the three-toned lipstick that had made Nick so furious during filming.

Well, sure enough, you couldn't see the courthouse for the flashbulbs when I made my first entrance in front of the building — and I sincerely hoped that the judge wouldn't be able to see the forest for the trees!

But on the way to the courthouse I had to endure the most stupendous horror. I saw a woman knocked over by a car. She was young and fashionable, and she was trying to run across the street with some bags from Macy's. It was the middle of summer and the weather was lovely and clear, but she was not crossing at a red light and a car turned from nowhere and hit her. I had a direct view of the whole thing from the cab. I heard her bones being crushed. And she died.

So there I am in the courtroom, after witnessing that. I was actually shaking, and I had cried a little, so the sunglasses were actually practical, not glamorous. Maybe it was all this that made it believable, but I probably would have been shaking and crying, anyway. Anyway, it all went off without a hitch, because, truth be told, we both just wanted to be rid of each other, and now we are rid of it all, the whole thing, even the threat of scandal. Because if Nick hasn't pillared me publicly yet, he isn't likely to do it now. So I am preparing to settle down. By that I don't mean get married again, God knows. Though I can't imagine myself unmarried, or at least without a man, and you can't be a movie star in Hollywood and not be married, because people *will talk*.

It seems to me that, quite regularly, absolutely nothing happens to me. My life is an endless array of non-incidents. My life lacks plot; particularly climax. I live in the cul-de-sac of a denouement to nothing. So when a situation does occur, when an incident does happen to me, I am quite unprepared for it. It's so shocking, to be acted upon, or involved with something, or asked to take an action myself. The incident with Lyon Jones was one such incident, but it was random enough for me to dismiss it, or at least not feel obligated to follow it up. I will remark that I did decide to cast Lyon, and Lyon did of course agree. It seemed to me that he might be right for my Venus.

I imagine Venus must have had large thighs, certainly in Boticcelli's version she does, and Lyon was certainly a virago, in the best sense of the word, with a lot of hair (only on his head, the rest of his body appears to be quite smooth), and quite sexually aggressive. Well, truth be told, I was interested in seeing Lyon naked (or did you guess that?), and I couldn't imagine that the audience would not enjoy that, too. I am reminded of the fact that most of the Restoration actresses were courtesans (attended to the king and the royalty no less), and they invited the audience to have sex with them after the play. Perhaps this could be worked into my scenarios somehow.

Anyway, the incident with Lyon was something that I took in my stride, not so much because it didn't matter that he had come on to me, but of course my real obsession had always been for someone else, remember? He had never left my mind. Pierre LeRoi, the boy in my class who had looked so much like Marky Mark, and who, I was still convinced, was at least as interested in me as I was in him. What I felt for Pierre could have been love, and I must admit that I certainly saw it that way and had always secretly nursed the fantasy that it might be. So no matter what was the outcome with Lyon (it's true what they say about the theatre, isn't it? About the performing arts? And the casting couch? One finds oneself surrounded by a bevy of eager beauty!) the one I was really waiting for was Pierre. And this whole gambit, this whole fiction (Would I ever direct a play? Was that in the cards, really?) was so that he might approach me again, after all these years — and offer himself up to me. For as I have said, it is not in my nature to chase after men, at least not in the ordinary way.

I want beauty to come to me (as unlikely as it sounds; but the incident with Lyon gives me hope that my strategy may work). It seems that is the only way that beauty can retain its integrity, for beauty coerced becomes ugly. That is perhaps the difference between love and desire, or rather the place where they must meet. If you lust after something and want to have sex with it — that is, if you need nothing but a body and would have sex with it, at any cost, in your fantasy only — then that is desire. But if you are waiting passively for beauty to fall into your arms — because one must never hurt beauty or do violence to it — then that is love. I never thought it would happen to me, and I am certainly quite capable of messing it up, but that is finally what has happened to me at the ripe old age of — well, let's just say I am approaching sixty-four.

So when I received an email from theking@istar.ca it struck me that *king* and *star* were both in one email address — but what struck me even more profoundly was that the email was most surely from *him*. I opened it up and I was excited by the mere arrogance of his email address. He calls himself *king*. How masterly.

I must say I have always been quite charmed by what some women see as sexism in males. And sexism is a bad thing for women — I'm not about to challenge hundreds of years of feminist activism. I suppose I am in the privileged position (that person at the arts council did instruct me to pay the world back for my privilege) of never being denied employment on the basis of my gender. But that is not entirely true; I can't imagine there is any profession other than academia that would embrace an old queen. (Of course, there's always hairdressing!)

But all that aside — let's leave civil law to the professionals — there is something pathetic about the masterly male, if one looks at him in a certain context. That is, if he is not raping you, or if you are not in danger of rape (I must admit that if I were to be raped, I would try my best to be compliant and get the most I could out of it!) then all this masterliness, all this kingship on the part of men — in other words all their imagined prowess and power — is pathetic and rather funny, and inevitably sexy. Look at how hard they try to personify all that they are cracked up to be. So the least we can do is offer them recompense for their performance anxiety (which I think is often more about their performance out of bed than in it) — that is, kiss them and allow ourselves to be fucked. (If I may stray from euphemism, for a moment.)

So there it was, in the undeniable fine print of an email address, Pierre LeRoi called himself the king, and so certainly he might be. I would be the last one to deny him that. Paradoxically (and paradox is nothing if not Shakespearean), what followed was peerless in its humility.

> Dear Doctor Moulton,
> I don't know if you remember me. I was in your fourth year Shakespeare class a long time ago (I think it's been 7 years). If you don't mind I would like to take the liberty of asking you if it might be alright if I auditioned for your play. It sounds fascinating,

and I've always had a great deal of respect for your scholarship. Your class was one of my favourites at the university. If you don't think I would be right for any of the roles, just say so, and I won't bother you. Thanks for your reading this, anyway.

With much respect, Pierre LeRoi.

That was it. Brief and to the point but dripping with reverence. I find praise of any ilk quite embarrassing. I am overwhelmed by the inappropriateness of it all. That this beautiful boy — and undoubtedly he would still be beautiful — would respect me, and ask my forgiveness for having dared to respond to my email was astounding and intimidating. How would I live up to this admiration? There was nothing admirable about me.

It did strike me, however, that this proposition would be an excuse to have lunch. So I emailed him back quite tersely — but certainly not impolitely — and suggested that we meet the next week; he seemed frighteningly available. Who would this young man be, who met me at lunch? My heart was literally in my mouth. If and when the luncheon might come, I did not know how I would speak.

* * * * * *

You might well ask me what I am doing running around with Cy Howard. I have wondered it, too. I hope it's not a rebound — he is in some ways a "Nick light." But he is certainly his own man, and I have never been with a man who wasn't. What does that mean exactly? It means that every man I have ever been with is a force of nature, a personality so volcanic that it's all I can manage to do to stay out of their way. I, too, have been called volcanic, and the situation right now is certainly not boring. I was shoehorned somehow into *Sudden Fear*, where I shall play the mistress yet again. Well, thank heavens for small somethings. I need an income because I stated quite clearly in the divorce that I have one — and that situation is reflected in the alimony. So I am doing it, there is no doubt about that, and having it off with Jack Palance at the same time.

Having it off would seem the requisite phrase. I don't know how to describe what's happening. Jack is such a *man*, that's the only way to describe him. He's quite irresistible and crazy for pushups — and it's charmingly erotic to watch him, before the shoot every day, being chided and kidded over his daily ritual: pushups on the sound-stage rug. His body is so lean and taut. I describe it in detail because he works so hard on it and is so proud of it, thus it seems an absolute necessity to praise it. And then there's that shock of straight, dark hair that falls not quite so accidentally over his forehead, so that he can keep brushing it carelessly off. And that jaw — which is too large for him to be truly handsome but nevertheless is very, very compelling. He's a lean animal; a kind of Adonis.

Though it's hard to imagine him being pierced in the thigh — he would insist on doing the piercing.

I have to admit that though he is gorgeous, I am with him not for that, but for the most awful reason really, and it's something I have never done before and swear I never will again. But it was clear at the first reading that Crawford wanted him; she's ever so clumsy about it. She would — yes, quite literally — get clumsy and drop things, and say, "Oh, Jack dear, could you pick them up" — her glasses or whatever, and then clasp his hand in hers, and say, "You're such a dear" and lick her lips. If you can imagine. And she is, I suppose, still desirable, in a way — if simply from sheer force of will. Well it's not enough that I *play* a woman who is stealing her husband, I just felt I had to steal Jack Palance. But that's not true. I really wanted him. What's not to want? Let's just say it added a bit of air to my balloon to drive Crawford crazy at the same time. She's such a bully that you can't not enjoy testing her and pushing her to the limit. She's had me barred from the set several days and I just adored it, I would dress up like a stagehand (how is that you might ask? well — with casual abandon, sunglasses verboten) and hide behind the set — now and then peering out from behind it hoping she would catch me. If she had seen me, I would just have said I forgot something and had to come by and pick it up; she would have had a fit and it would be so much fun watching her explode.

So it's one great adventure. But what I have with Jack is not permanent, he and I both know it. So I have been dating

Cy. I don't know what to say about him other than the fact that he is absolutely the funniest man I have ever met. He's a comedy writer, so of course this makes sense. And quite good looking, for a comedy writer. I knew that he would be a lot of fun in bed; that's never a problem, anyway. What I'm concerned about is that he keeps dropping hints about my career. Can you believe it? It's almost amusing how hopeless this cause is. Anyway, I swear that he is hinting that I am too career oriented. Well, I am, and not at all ashamed of it. I can feel an Oscar coming on, and to pretend that I wouldn't care one way or another would be a horrible lie (we all say that it's an honour to be nominated but deep down it's all we want). I know I am an actress, and for any actress worth her salt it's the award that makes life worth living.

I don't think I'll get it for this one, but people are saying lovely things about the rushes, and the sense is that after all these years for some reason (why does this suddenly happen?) people are beginning to take me seriously, and another Oscar nomination seems less an accident than simply inevitable. So I'm trying to just ignore the prodding on his part. (Not that kind of prodding, *that* kind of prodding I take quite seriously!) Because it doesn't matter; why should it? I will have my way, always have, can't see any reason not to.

There is one other odd thing about my life though. There are still letters from Tony. If he had his way, he would write me every week; he tried that, but I wouldn't have it. I only write him once a month, no matter what. His letters are very touching. He is growing up very quickly, or else he is trying to impress me — but either way, he has. He says that he wants to go into film. I used to think this was just to irritate his father, but now I'm thinking he might actually mean it. It's very different communicating with him. I would say it's friendship but — whenever I send a letter to him there is an image of him in front of me. I try not to call it up; but the image won't go away. Anyway, it's all different with him, as I say, it's calmer. And it would be a friendship, except that it still seems not to be. On his part, anyway, it's much more than that. I keep thinking of Noël Coward's *Private Lives* — my mother was in that play once in London, and I loved it so much. Coward was really onto something. The primary relationship in the play is so toxic but so damned appealing, and then when they're with lawfully wedded spouses it's so boring. But I mean, does it have to be like that? Just for fun, sometimes I fantasize about Tony and me. Not in bed, but just together. A kind of "permanent" together. All right, marriage! I know that sounds crazy, and we'll save the judgments for later. But I'm wondering if the opposite of Nick is Tony. Because that would be a bad thing, in a way. I really was in love with Nick, whatever that means, the same way as I am falling in love with Cy. But even with Cy, I wonder: Is there some sort of compromise? Is it really a case of either living a life that is mind-numbingly boring or one that involves going to the hospital now and then to mend the stitches? That is actually the fantasy I'm pondering at the moment. And I'm thinking that Cy's antagonism to my career might offer just the right amount of friction, to keep things exciting —

that is, beyond his incredible wit and his delightful prodding. We'll see.

And there's still Tony. But I can't think about him. Not now.

It's an ancient place. The waiters are ancient. I thought I would be comfortable here. If he had suggested one of those fancy trendy places with the wooden communal seating areas and the millennials texting each other across the table, it would have been a nightmare. Also, I won't look quite as out of place here as I do everywhere else. It's called Pratfalls, if you can believe it. I don't know who named it or why. I used to come here may years ago with an older lover who valued my assets when I had them. There is something vaguely elegant about it, but it is very plainly decorated. The waiters rush around in a hushed sort of way; they are not having more fun than you are (at least not visibly), which is what separates good service from bad in my humble opinion. I was early. It would have been more politic for me to be late, but I couldn't manage it. He was just slightly late, but this offered the opportunity for him to be ever so sorry. I couldn't believe it — but it made perfect sense — that he would look exactly the same. What also hadn't changed was my desire for him. He set off all the same electric shocks in me as before, so many years ago. Quiet intensity, mixed with — there is an air of integrity about him, as if he is a very right-thinking young man. I remembered that when we took the bus together he used to exit at a boring suburb called Erin Parkway, where he undoubtedly lived with his parents. How could so much earnest beauty arise from the suburbs? But the suburbs couldn't contain him and that's why he was lunching with me.

He was wearing a leather jacket and a sweater, zipper undone and dark in colour, over a light-coloured tank top that revealed some very pale and appealing chest skin. As he apologized profusely he removed the leather jacket, and I was so subsumed with the prospect of his removing the sweater and sitting opposite me in that fetching tank top that at first I didn't notice. But then he did not, to my surprise, remove the sweater.

And then I realized. Pierre was wearing *my sweater*. The one I thought had gone missing in the classroom, remember? I couldn't quite believe my eyes. He folded his hands on the table and leaned toward me. He didn't seem conscious that he was wearing my sweater, but I couldn't let the elephant remain in the room unacknowledged. "As I say, I'm SO sorry to be late."

"You've apologized enough," I said.

"Have I apologized too much?" he asked earnestly. I remembered now the kind of verbal merry-go-rounds we often engaged in, because Pierre tended to be so apologetic with me in any circumstance that any actual mistake on his part brought a deluge of "I'm sorrys" and self-justification. I stopped it.

"You're wearing my sweater," I said. And then realized that yet again this might mean another apology. Strangely, it didn't.

"Yes. I have to explain about that," he said.

"I think you should," I said. "I had to make my trek to the bus without it on a very windy evening."

"Yes. I'm sorry about that —" but he appeared less sorry than he was eager to explain. "I guess I'd better let the cat out of the bag." Everything about him was anachronistic, including that statement. Who said that anymore? He was like the romantic ideal of a young man from another era, he even spoke in pre–Holden Caulfield Tin-Pan-Alley slang. "I was, I guess, in my undergraduate days, I was ... well, I was pretty obsessed with you."

I said: "Why, I don't know what you mean," quite expressionlessly — it was meant to be coy.

"What I mean is" — he leaned forward, even more earnestly — "I respect you, Dr. Moulton. I really respect you. Your learning, your ideas, and, I have to say it, I respect the stand you take about your sexuality."

I told him I wasn't aware that I was making any sort of stand.

"Oh, but you did, you did. None of the other teachers ever talk about being gay."

"Well, you must have other gay professors."

"Oh, sure. Lots," he said. "But they never talk about it, they always treated it like a dirty secret — but you never did.

I really respected that. I mean, really. And — and I still do."
He was still completely the same, earnest, honest Pierre.

"And so you stole my sweater …?" I left the question dangling.

"Yes. Yes I did. It was a pretty stupid thing to do, but I guess I just couldn't say goodbye." Did he say what I think he had just said? "And so, when I saw the ad for your play I couldn't believe it. I mean, I hadn't forgotten about you after all these years. I couldn't get you out of my mind. And I just thought, this is a chance to see him again."

"I hope you're not stalking me," I said, with false sternness, trying to make light of the situation.

"Well — yeah, I kind of am." He laughed and then saw my alarm. "But not in a bad way. I mean, well … I admire you a lot, that's all."

"Is that all?" I said. I couldn't resist. It was reckless of me. I was inviting a door slammed in my face.

"Well, I don't know what it means. I just — well, I like you a lot Dr. Moulton. And I missed you. That's all." He was staring at me.

I picked up my menu. "Shouldn't we look at the menu?" It left me a minute to think. What to do? I didn't know what was going on. I couldn't believe what he was saying. It was a dream come true. First Lyon and now this. Why were my ex-students throwing themselves at me all of a sudden? Was it all over something as stupid as a little audition? Whoever said theatre was dead didn't know what he was talking about! Or had my old man's luck suddenly changed? I became intensely anxious. I put down the menu and stood up. I didn't know what I was doing exactly, and the room began to reel just enough to make me want to sit down. But I didn't. "Pierre," I said.

"Yes?" he said. He got up, too.

"I wonder if you would mind if I left."

"Oh. I'm sorry. Is it something I — is it the sweater?"

"No, not at all." Just enormous anxiety, is what I wanted to say. "No, it's not that. I ... I didn't feel well this morning and I came out, anyway, but could we make it another time ... this discussion? Perhaps ... of an evening?" What an odd turn of phrase. Listening to myself, I didn't even believe that I had said that.

"Of course. Are you all right?"

"Yes, I'll be just fine." I grabbed my coat from the back of the chair. I knew exactly what was causing the anxiety. Suddenly, I was going to get everything I wanted — the boy I was in love with was obviously throwing himself at me, there was no doubt about that, and I was going to have him star in my dream production of *Venus and Adonis*, and he was going to play Adonis. Pierre would be Adonis both in my dreams and my life. It was all too much for me. I told him to email me the next day, left a ten-dollar tip for nothing, and rushed out of the restaurant.

*   *   *   *   *   *

I don't like this. I don't like it at all. I should be happy but
I'm not. Normally, I wouldn't be bothered. I shouldn't be
bothered. Okay. This is what has happened. All of a sudden
Tony is talking to his father again. I shouldn't find this upsetting. This should be something that I want. But why all of a
sudden?

The stated reason makes no sense at all. He wants Tony to
help him as assistant director on his new film *Rebel Without
a Cause* (that is the working title) — the property that he
mentioned so many years ago at the party with the writer
Maxwell Shane. *Rebel Without a Cause* is another movie
about juvenile delinquents, apparently. But Tony is not a juvenile delinquent. Except, of course, for that incident with
me, but that hardly qualifies. So why all of a sudden out of
the blue? The fact is I am jealous — all right, I admit it — and
there's nothing I can do about it. I could ask why, but there
we go again — where is that sort of analysis going to get me?
Well it's obvious, anyway, my whole relationship with Tony
is based on the fact that we bonded over our difficulties with
Nick, so if suddenly Tony has no difficulties with Nick then
Tony and I will have no relationship. But honestly, am I that
shallow that I can't celebrate the reunion of father and son
because it might disadvantage *me*? What's worse though —
am I that deeply emotionally involved with Tony after more
than two years have passed since *the incident*?

I can't believe I'm talking about this. I can't believe I'm
thinking about this. I should be glad; Tony loves his father
and is overjoyed about the fact that he has a chance to patch

up their relationship. If I was a good ex-stepmother, I would be happy for him. Maybe this just explains that I never ever was a stepmother to him at all. But, Jesus, why I am so bleeding angry?

The events just keep happening. I longed for a life crowded with incident and now there are too many. I should be happy, I suppose. Of course I should be happy; that's the whole point. Isn't it? Perhaps there was another point all along. Perhaps the point of everyone's life is not to be happy but to be unhappy. People wonder why they have so many unrealized dreams. Chekhov is all about this, Shakespeare glances at this, as he glances at everything — but why? Is it because we are deluded into thinking that we actually want to be happy when we actually want to be unhappy? That sounds insane.

What I mean is that we cannot stand happiness — at least not for too long — untainted with tragedy, because we are creatures of death and know we are all going to die. This doesn't explain suburbia, the middle classes — the vast tracts of numbing witlessness that characterizes the lives of most people who seem to find happiness. But no, that is contentment, not happiness.

That's it — contentment is not threatening. Only unbridled happiness threatens us with its promise of perfection. I have been content for many years planning my own suicide — variously, quickly and then slowing down and then speeding up again — but always it seems that the equilibrium for me has been to be in a state in which I am always at the point of failing at everything, though never quite do. The sudden realization of all my dreams — which of course cannot be happening — seems to have only one remedy. So I rushed out of Pratfalls (aptly named — a sublime setting for mishaps and mischances) and went directly to the gay bookstore.

This was insane, I never go there. The place is a sad commentary on where we have all come to. It's now a coffee-shop restaurant during the day and pop-up bar at night, and they've moved the books to the back, and they never dust the shelves. The staff is insanely uninformed about what books they do or do not have. No one who goes in there seems to know that it is a bookstore, the millennials and some sad older types come there for the coffee and the booze. Except for me. I actually do browse the somewhat ancient tomes they have on display. So I feel safe there.

I entered the bookstore and there was a young man there who I had seen before. I haven't mentioned this particular young man. I met him — well, we did not actually meet — at the pre-bar that I attend before I make my presence known in the dark room. As I say, no one ever looks at me at that bar (or anywhere in the light, as I am a cockroach on carrion, a *doodlebug of the dark*), so it was astounding to me that this young man, at one point, did. He had an astounding look, too — long black hair with a shock of it that he keeps lifting with a concerted casualness away from his deep dark eyes, and western-style cowboy boots with fashionably distressed jeans, and, when I saw him in winter, a massive fur winter coat. His skin was very dark (he was not, however, Black) and he looked like the kind of man who would get a five o'clock shadow at eight in the morning. Well, anyway, this young man looked at me. And I looked back at him. And we played the staring game for a while in the bar. It was so bewitching for me that I didn't go to the dark room, I left the bar in order to see what would happen. He followed me. We made our way to the next street corner and then we looked at each other. And then I turned and left.

It was all too unlikely for words; I had just run away from Pierre, my heart thumping, and now here he was. The same game began again — he looked at me, I looked at him. It just seemed that everything in my life was changing; was I wearing a new mask? Had the Gods blessed me by taking away fifty years of wrinkles? Not likely. Whatever. I would do something so unlike me, I would act. I said hello to him, and he said hello back. He asked me what I was up to. Obviously a sexual invitation. I didn't know what to do. I told him I was going to a movie. He asked if he could go, too. This was crazy. Go with it. I said: let's do it. (I was running from something; I didn't know at the time, but it was all the good things that seemed to be happening to me. I had to somehow throw a wrench in the works. I realize now that this young man looked like the one to do it. We went outside and I got us a cab. The movie was *The Disaster Artist*, about the creator of the camp film *The Room*, and it starred James Franco. I was thinking of going to that movie, anyway; I love movies about the making of movies — imagining the sound sets and what goes on backstage.

I thought, *This is insane. I'm going to a movie with a beautiful young man who wants to have sex with me when I am in love with Pierre, and he is in love with me. What is happening?* Well, anyway, so went my screwball thoughts, I might as well go to a film I would actually enjoy. As soon as we were alone in the cab we continued looking at each other. He was so darkly handsome. I began to question him about his life; he told me he was a recent Italian immigrant. He certainly looked like a refugee from a Pasolini movie; I imagined that the boys who killed the famous gay Italian filmmaker must have looked like him. (Did you know that the young man who killed Pasolini had a last name which, in English, means *frog*? Irrelevant, I know.) He said that he was a construction worker (this, again, I could believe; he had massive biceps and massive, hairy man-hands) and was presently out of work so he had time for a movie. *I'll pay*, I thought, *I'll do him a favour, he's down and out.*

When we got to the movie I realized they had a bar — as most movie theatres do now, trying to lure people out of their homes with alcohol. I offered to buy him a drink. I thought: *I must be drunk for this, whatever it is.* We sat there and he complimented me on my hairless arm. I told him that the grass is only greener because he is hairy. I must confess that by this time I had what can only be called an unrelenting boner in my pants (you may, at this point, long for the usual euphemisms!) — or as much of a "boner" as an old man like me can have. I desired him so much. This would certainly throw a wrench into everything with Pierre. Was I in love with this boy now, or was I still in love with Pierre, and what was I to do about Lyon, anyway? I was dizzy with desire. I was sure that we would have sex during the movie or at least I would blow him, so when we got into the theatre I dragged him into the top row. I was very annoyed to suddenly realize that there was a couple sitting quite near us. Well, what did that matter. I could still blow him in the dark — the dark that I am so used to. It took a very long time for the lights to completely go down in the theatre and the film to start. When it did I immediately grabbed his giant hand and started to caress the inside of it, and he caressed my hand in return. It was so incredibly erotic. And then my hand slipped down to his thigh, and I basically spent the whole movie with my hand there, but I was too frightened to actually feel his crotch. It was intoxicating. I was high on sex, and we hadn't even had it yet. When we left the movie I felt like dinner, so I suggested we have some. He said that he was very hungry.

This was odd to me. Could he not afford a meal? Did he still have that beautiful winter fur coat? If so, why not sell it? But I didn't say anything, and I didn't think much of it. I, of course, offered to pay for the meal, and once he got it he started wolfing it down. How long had it been since he had eaten?

Then began his tremendous speech. It was Shakespearean in its sudden volubility — very unlike this silent young man with the dark eyes. "I am so sorry, I must apologize," he said. "I feel so sorry that you are paying for this meal for me. This is not a regular thing for me. When I get a job, I must pay you back. I feel I owe you this money. It is very kind of you, but it makes me feel very bad about myself. I do not wish to — how do you say it? — mooch with you. That is not nice. You are very nice to me, but you are too nice, and I feel very bad about doing this. I promise, I will pay you back. It is not like me to do this. Not like me at all. I am not like this."

I told him to relax and eat his dinner, but he would not relent. "I must tell you that I am very, very sorry."

"There's no need to be sorry," I said. "It will just give you indigestion."

He cleared his plate — he vacuumed it. I desired him so much. I stood up. I wanted to kiss him. No one was near this corner of the restaurant, it was kind of a straight singles bar/restaurant but the evening trade had not arrived as of yet. He said thank you and went to hug me, and I raised my lips to his.

He wouldn't kiss me, but he hugged me for a long while. When we separated he said, "You are excited, no?" I told him that yes I was excited. Boy, was I excited.

"I can feel it," he said, with a shy smile. And then it happened. We were outside the restaurant. I was realizing that I was not entirely comfortable with him for some reason and I did not know why. He made me understand. "I'm going through a hard time," he said.

"Oh?" I said.

"Yes. I have a friend who lends me money, but he's away for the weekend. He's coming back on Monday. So I don't have any money to get me through the next two days. I just need a little money to pull me through. I don't know how I'm going to get it.'"

Then it hit me, like a thunderclap. He was a hooker, what is politely called a sex-trade worker, but there was nothing polite about this. I had been duped. I was a very sad, old man indeed, because I had imagined that he was attracted to me. No one could ever be attracted to me again; not him, not Pierre or Lyon, they simply wanted parts in my play, and I was an elderly letch taking advantage of their youth, naïveté, and beauty. I felt lower than the ground. I hated this young man. Was he even really Italian?

I smiled somehow and said goodbye, and he followed me. I got into a cab. He followed me into the cab. I couldn't help it. I put my hand on his thigh again, talked about the weather. But I knew what he was now, I had entered a zone where I could not feel desire, just humiliation and defeat.

I stopped the cab near a local bathhouse that I know very well. I used to go there; now I am too old to go anywhere where beauty is. Nevertheless I sprinted out as best an old man can. I left "Luigi" in the cab; he would have to pay for it. Maybe he could have sex with the cab driver. I know this was cruel of me, but I now had lost all control.

Inside the bathhouse I very carefully took off all my clothes and placed them high up in the locker in a plastic bag that is provided for shoes. I had heard that this bathhouse had bedbugs and even though I was on what seemed to be a suicide mission, that didn't stop me from being careful.

I went to an adjacent room to have a shower. A young man was standing in the shower. He was extraordinarily beautiful — as now, it seems to me, all young men are. I did not look at him. It was not my place. I could never look beauty in the face ever again. I did glance over my shoulder at him though. He had decided to pee in the shower. The golden stream was strong and seemed never-ending. I sat down on the shower floor with some difficulty (I have a very bad back), and the stream was still going. I opened my mouth in his direction. He knew what to do. He came over to me and with some satisfaction peed directly into my mouth. There was so much that I almost choked. But it tasted good, so very warm and comforting. I let it wash all over me. It was comforting because I realized that I was doing the right thing, that I was acting as the Gods wished. I was connecting with this boy in the way that was the only way for me now. I was letting beauty pee on me, and keeping my distance. It was delicious.

I know I shouldn't be satisfied now. And satisfaction is not the right word; it's wrong for me to be happy. I'm not happy. I'm not contented, either, I'm just … I'm distressed for Tony because it didn't all work out. I knew somehow, deep down, it wouldn't, but the depravity of that man — my ex-husband, Mr. Nicholas Ray — must never be underestimated.

So it turns out it was all a ruse. All a lie. And it just confirms what I always thought about Nick: that underneath it all he is a pervert. Not that homosexuals are perverts, not all of them, that is, I've met some very nice ones in my time — the ones who have somehow managed to be who they are — though I can't imagine what their lives would be like. Nick, however, is — and I think this ruination of a situation proves it — a one hundred percent homosexual, deep down.

Now it occurs to me that he was probably pummelling me because that was the only way he could keep his erection, pardon my French, and he hated my desire not because he was jealous of the men I was flirting with, but because I got to flirt with them and he didn't. Tony told me what happened between him and his father, on the phone. Yes, he phoned me, and yes, I answered; he asked for my phone number in a letter — for an emergency — and I gave it to him. He's almost seventeen now. Almost (but not quite) an adult. I won't meet with him because I have a feeling that I know what would happen. But I can't *not* communicate with him. He has weirdly become a part of my emotional life; that's just the way it is.

So, Nick flew him to Hollywood (Tony has been living at the pre-college he is now attending), supposedly because Nick — all of a sudden, out of the blue— wanted to encourage his first son's film career. I thought this whole project to be an unlikely one from the beginning, but because Tony's heart was so set on it, I refused to be a negative Nancy. I said things like, "He loved you all along, like I said he did," and "There's no reason why you can't become a filmmaker like your father. He'll be the best teacher in the world, he absolutely loves film." I said all this feeling I might well rue the day. And indeed I do. No, I'm not sorry. I was obligated to encourage him at the time, it would have been cruel not to. So he arrived at the studio and became Nick's assistant and, of course, hung around with all the young people — Natalie Wood, James Dean, and Sal Mineo — who are close to his own age.

Now it should be stated at the outset what this film is actually about. I had been told it was about juvenile delinquents, and it ostensibly is — that is certainly what will sell the movie as juvenile delinquents are definitely all the rage these days — but that's not what the film is actually about. The film is actually about a young man's relationship with his father. (I have sources.) Apparently, the big scene comes when James Dean's character has a sit-down with his pa and tries to force the old man, who is described in the script as being "stiff necked" (I can't think of a more appropriate term for Nick's perennial posture than "stiff necked"). The boy's father is incapable of expressing emotion.

The same obviously applies to Nick's relationship with Tony. So it's important to understand that Nick asked Tony down to Hollywood to help him with a film that is, essentially, *about their relationship*. So already we're in tricky territory. It reminds me very much of "our" movie — since Nick has decreed I not call it "our" movie ever again, I will — when

Nick decided to try and perform the relationship I had with Humphrey Bogart in the movie in our real life. If he starts to do this with Tony, it will be nothing but torture for the boy. Who knows what an emotional quagmire such a situation might cause? Well, to make a long story short, it did. Tony immediately bonded with Sal Mineo, who is a very nice person (very dark and Latin looking, with puppy-dog eyes) and almost exactly his age (but homosexual, apparently). However, Tony began to realize that Nick was pushing him to spend more time with James Dean.

This was not a big issue for Tony at first. James Dean is obviously a very attractive and charismatic young man; he is becoming an icon of sorts, and it may be because of his beautiful wavy hair and twinkling eyes, luscious lips, and firm, straight jaw. But the key is that Nick was not getting along so well with this budding icon. It isn't that they hated each other — they were functioning as actor and director — but Nick didn't as yet feel close enough to James Dean for what he had in mind. That is the phrase that Tony used, quoting his father, "close enough." I asked him what Nick meant by that and Tony said he meant "artistically" close. But you must understand that with Mr. Nicholas Ray, artistically close just means *close*, there really is no other level with him — as film is the only thing he cares about. Specifically, Tony asked Nick to ferret out some details about James's private life.

James Dean is a hard nut to crack; of course, everyone wants him. I know, to some extent, what kind of pressure that can put on a person. He seems profound to all who meet him, profound and sweet, with a brooding edge. Ergo, no one really seems to know who James Dean is sleeping with at any given moment. There are people in and out of his life but he's a free spirit, plays the bongos, apparently, reads Zen poetry, and is just, well, generally hard to pin down.

Now, I found it very disturbing that Nick asked Tony to find out about James Dean's sex life — because that's what he meant by "private life," of course. On the one hand, this sounds like a classic method acting approach, which is why I don't like method acting; it can be intrusive and mishandled and people can go literally crazy with it. The good-old British method is good enough for me. Basically, it's all about learning your lines and not bumping into furniture — just kidding, that was Noël Coward again! No, it's about creating characters — certainly — but it's also about simply understanding your objectives. I mean there is no need to *psychoanalyze*.

So here is Nick asking Tony to play sleuth about James Dean's private bedroom activities. The first thing that occurred to me: was Nick trying to get Tony to sleep with James? I wouldn't put it past him. Was the voyeur in him hoping to get the juicy details about James Dean, naked, in bed, having sex with his own son? Again, it all seems quite possible to me. Nick would do anything to make his film perfect, but it does strike me that — and this is the alarming part — there is not any good reason that I can think of why he would have to know about James Dean's sex life in order to make this film.

And here it gets very strange, because Tony retrieved the usual information — it involved various women, various one-night stands that James Dean was involved with, his first girlfriend back in Indiana, that sort of thing. He brought this information but that was not enough. Nick wanted more. And it turns out he wanted more information of a specific kind. He wanted to know if James Dean had ever had any homosexual experiences. (Aha!)

Of course, Tony dutifully went back and got Dean drunk and finally, still with some awkwardness, dragged a juicy detail out of him. It turns out that James Dean is bisexual, and that his own particular thrill (and please don't judge me for judging James Dean, I'm not) was to have men — at some homosexual sex party apparently — (are you sitting down?) put out their cigarettes on him. Can you believe it? He wished to be a human ashtray. Well, that's the kind of dirt you discover when you go fishing about in other people's business, putting your nose where it shouldn't be; you learn things you'd rather not know. I don't know if this human ashtray business is true. I trust Tony, but I don't know James Dean well enough to know whether he was pulling Tony's leg. Tony is obviously naive in these matters, so he may have been leading the boy down the garden path; it would certainly be a fine joke on Dean's part to make fun of Tony's job as private sex investigator. Whatever.

So Tony runs back to tell Nick and Nick just laps this up. But it is not enough. No, he must have more. Now his motives become somewhat more clear. It turns out that the Sal Mineo character in the film (Plato, i.e., Platonic love, i.e., Greek love) is — according to Nick, anyway — a homosexual character.

This makes sense. Sal Mineo, the actor who plays the part, is a lovely, dreamy-eyed young man, very fragile and vulnerable, and he is apparently gay, but homosexuality is never explicitly referred to in the script. Instead the relationship with Dean and Mineo is kind of a brotherly friendship, with Dean hugging the weak and defenceless Sal Mineo in a comforting way. Was it because of Nick's own perverted hidden obsessions that he wanted so desperately to make the relationship between Dean and Mineo's characters so explicit? If only he were to leave the film as it is, wouldn't this be the kind of interpretive detail about the movie that elderly, professorial, homosexual film critics might enjoy ferreting out?

But no — the way the script subtly portrays the relationship between these two boys is not enough for Nick. He wants to film a scene where Dean kisses Mineo on the lips. *On the lips.* Oh dear me, is he insane? Of course the studio would never allow this scene to be included in the final cut. But that doesn't stop Nick — in these situations nothing will. So he suggests that Tony get very drunk with Sal Mineo and James Dean and then instigate a party game in which the two actors in the film pretend to be fags, and thus get Sal and James to kiss.

Tony is skeptical, but how skeptical can he be to his father's face? For Nick is the man he idolizes, the man whose admiration he craves more than anything. So Tony agrees to try and have the party and get Sal and Dean together, and get them to do something nasty with each other, as Nick would stand for absolutely nothing less. What was initially a request for his son to do him a favour, of course, became a demand from Nick, the tyrannical father: "No. Don't *just try*. That's not good enough. Get it done."

So now Tony is terrified; in order to keep his father's love, he has to force this homosexual moment on Dean and Sal, who are now his friends and trust him. He doesn't want to do it, but he loves his father. At this moment, it should have been clear to Tony that his father didn't invite him down because he loved him, or because he wanted to teach him about filmmaking, but for one reason only — because he needed someone who could facilitate the big homosexual *scènes à faire* he so desired. (Or did he desire it for other than filmic reasons?) He needed a young man nearer the age of Sal Mineo and James Dean who could befriend them and manipulate them in his stead.

Tony arranged the drunken evening, and everyone was very sloshed. He told me that it was agony for him; but that he finally got up the courage to suggest a party game — that James and Sal might dare each other to kiss. The moment he said it, he knew that it had been the wrong thing to say; that he had dropped a bomb in the room. Suddenly, Dean and Sal were very uncomfortable — hemming and hawing and flashing suspicious looks at him. Of course, now they thought Tony was gay; that he was trying to manipulate them into performing a gay act in front of him. Tony was humiliated and immediately changed the subject — hoping his suggestion would be forgotten. But nothing was ever right again that night. And after that Dean and Sal no longer trusted Tony as a friend — and never would again.

But that was only the beginning. Then Tony had to tell his father the idea didn't quite work out. That was the most dreadful moment of all, because inevitably Nick lost his noodle and screamed at him, accused him of ruining his movie, and said that now it would be impossible to film the scene. Tony was devastated. And then his father wouldn't speak to him, and he had nothing to do on the set. He wandered about, evidently useless, terribly embarrassed, because now neither the crew nor the other actors could understand why he was there — other than because he was Nicholas Ray's son. Horrible. (And now it turns out that Nick has somehow gotten James Dean and Sal Mineo to do the kissing scene and is having a big fight with the studio about whether or not to actually include it in the film.) But when it comes to Tony, Nick has simply forgotten that his son is there, or apparently even that he is alive.

I told Tony that he should make a promise to himself — like I did — never to go anywhere near Nick in the future, ever. This has become a bond between us once again, our mutual promise. Believe it or not — despite the horrors Tony has been through — I don't know if I have entirely convinced him to banish his father from his life. It would certainly be difficult to say goodbye to your own father forever.

Tony's half-brother (and my own son), Timmy, is only five years old (and I have custody) but that might not stop Nick from trying to lure him away from me the way he lured Tony away — briefly yet catastrophically. It worries me endlessly that Timmy will ask to live with his father when he gets older. I would now have no second thoughts about simply saying, in no uncertain terms, "That would not be a good idea!" The man is so incredibly toxic that both his sons should stay permanently away from him. And right now it would be self-destructive for Tony to do anything else.

My heart went out to Tony on the phone. I wanted so desperately to see him, to hug him, to make it better. But I decided, wisely I think, to wait.

Dinner was set for eight o'clock. It was 7:30 and I had chopped all the vegetables. It was to be coq au vin; it's the only thing I can cook. In addition, the name of the dish is a pun, which puts us in vaguely Shakespearean territory.

I was terrified. I was on a suicide mission and I knew it. But there was only one way to be, one way to act. I had decided on my code of conduct after my encounter with the hooker and at the baths. I had been running from the truth too long. The fact was that I am not worthy. I am not worthy of the love of a young man even if he wanted to love me. I am too old. Much too old and ugly. If a young man were to love me it would be because he himself was demented, or because I had dragged himself into some dementia of my own. I am like one of the witches in *Macbeth*, somewhat toothless (I wear a bridge) and a woman with a beard (that's what I am really, let's be honest). To imagine that I could be loved by a young man would be to put a spell on him, would be to bewitch language, the way the witches do in *Macbeth*. What kind of perversion would that be — of the word love? I know where my place is: lower than the ground, because liquids sink into the ground, and that's where I belong.

It would make sense on one level to just commit suicide. A double suicide occurred to me — I could have poisoned the meal — but that would not be fair. What I was planning was a double suicide *of a kind* and that would be unfair enough.

Still, I could not believe that Pierre wanted me, in that way. However, now I was prepared.

The thing about coq au vin is that you have to cook it in the presence of your guest, and let it simmer, so this gave me something to do. Pierre arrived just on time. He was dressed in the sweater that he stole from me, but he quickly removed that and was only wearing a tank top, a different one than when I had met him before. His arms were exquisite. I didn't remember him actually doing that in class — that is, exposing his arms like that, his vulnerable flesh. His arms were so white and soft looking, I wanted to sink my teeth into him like a cannibal. Well, certainly I was Caliban, cooking up a meal. He didn't have gigantic muscles, that Pierre, not as big as the real Marky Mark, but he did have muscles and they just seemed so inappropriate hiding within that tender flesh, pressing gently against the casing of his skin; he was bursting with vitality. I wanted inside him.

No, I would have him inside me, in a way. Yes, I certainly would.

I told him that I would have to cook and chat with him at the same time, because that is the way coq au vin is done. He didn't seem to mind. At first it was all about how odd it was for him to observe his professor cooking. He never imagined I cooked. "Oh, I do lots of things," I said flirtatiously. I could flirt with him now. Now that I was going to be lower than the ground for him, anything was possible.

"Oh, I see," he said, somewhat awkwardly, but only because he was trying to figure out a way to flirt back. "What kind of other things do you do?" he said, which was not particularly witty, but very flirty.

"Oh, that's for me to know and you to find out," I said, continuing in the same vein. I was ridiculous, I was Don Pasquale in Donizetti's opera of the same name, the fat, ugly old man who is so vain that he imagines he can be loved by a young girl, and Pierre was Norina, the teenager who teaches him a lesson. But I was going to teach us both a lesson. "I hope it's all right that you see me doing ordinary things."

"I'd like to see you do even more ordinary things," he said, letting the cat out of the bag, as if it wasn't out of the bag already. Well, he wanted me, he wanted me as much as I wanted him, but I couldn't let it happen. I was like the priest in the movie *Harold and Maude*, who speaks with such detestation about the vision of young and old flesh co-mingling. It was not right. It was a sin that his tender flushed paleness should come near to my too tanned old wrinkles. (Yes, I do the tanning machine occasionally, that's how hopeless I am; well, now I will have to stop even that.)

Then it was important for me to focus on the meal, so I let him ramble on. "It's amazing how you think your professor can't be an ordinary person. I guess I kind of idolized you in a way, I'm not afraid to say it. I just never met anyone like you. When you told us how old you were, I just couldn't believe it. I don't believe it, actually. You're not that old. And age doesn't mean anything, anyway." So he had reached for that cliche, the cliche of cliches, the ultimate hiding place for the deluded young lover who refuses to accept the truth. Of course, age means *everything*. Certainly, we are all going to die, but some of us sooner than others, and that makes all the difference in the world. You are either on your way in or on your way out, and to pretend that you are on your way in when you are not is just futile and denying life itself, because life is just a prelude to death, but when we're young and beautiful we are able, for a time, to forget about all that. I wanted to contradict him but I thought, *Why bother?* He will be contradicted, anyway, and I might as well let him live in his little fantasy world a few minutes longer. "I'm just saying, it's odd because I actually idolized you so much that I thought you were a kind of a God."

"A God," I said. This did perplex me. "You mean like Venus in *Venus and Adonis*?"

"No — not like that." No, he would not want to think about that. He didn't want to be gored by a boar. "More like Zeus and Ganymede."

Of course, that would be his fantasy. I was thinking now about all the lectures I had given about Ganymede — the beautiful boy who Zeus captured in order to make him immortal (and Ganymede's Latin name Catamitus provided the early modern term *catamite* — precursor of the modern term *homosexual*). How it must have excited him to find a place for himself in all of this. I had been proselytizing — now I could see that all of my teaching had been proselytizing — I was what everyone feared, I was the homosexual who could turn you into one. Well certainly Pierre must have been a homosexual before he met me, but now what had happened, and I never thought it would, was that I had managed to create an acolyte, a worshipper, who was using the very image that I implanted in his mind as teacher to manipulate him into loving me. I had done all this. Well, it would be undone. "I hope you like bacon," I said. "I hope you're not one of those horrible vegetarians. I should have asked you first."

"I can smell the bacon," he said, "and I like it. I can't wait."

"We'll get fat together," I said.

"Oh, you're not fat," he said. And I could see what it would be, our future, if I was to allow it to happen. How hard he would have to work to make me feel desirable. But how could I ever feel desirable if I was only desirable in his eyes and not my own? How could I ever believe him if I couldn't believe myself? I served up the meal and it was a real culinary triumph; the mixture of wine, bacon, mushrooms, and thyme gives it such a tasty herbal tang. He ate it in a leisurely fashion. I could see that he was still getting used to the fact that his professor, a God, was having a meal with him. I remembered the time when he got me a coffee, and I was afraid to have him prepare it the way I wanted because I was afraid to say, to him, the word *cream*. How times had changed.

When we finished, I offered him a glass of wine and I suggested that we retire to my living room. He sat on the couch. I thought it was best to come quickly to the climax of our evening. I had removed the living-room rug. The floor looked somewhat bare but it was necessary. I sat down at his feet next to a rather ratty old leatherette stool I had bought specifically for the occasion. I leaned on the stool, with some difficulty wrapping my legs underneath me on the floor. "Oh, you're sitting on the floor?" he said, somewhat uncomfortably.

And I told him yes. He would have to deal with it. "I like to be lower than low," I said. He didn't know how to deal with this. He sipped his wine so politely. His arms. "I want to ask you a favour," I said.

"Sure," he shrugged.

"I'd like you to pull down your pants."

"Oh, yeah?" he said. But he wasn't overly perturbed. I could tell it was something he'd be glad to do. "Ahh, sure."

"I want to look at you," I said.

"Okay," he said, amenable. He stood up and let his pants drop to the floor. "My underwear?" he asked, referring to the tighty-whities that were staring me in the face.

"Yes, please," I said, in my best old schoolmarm's voice, "them, too." He let them drop before. It was lovely, of course. Very thick, nestled there. He didn't shave his balls. I knew what I wanted and what it was incumbent on me to do. "I want you to pee on me," I said.

"What?" he said. It was the first time I had seen him truly discombobulated since he had entered my apartment.

"Pee on me. Into my mouth." I opened up my mouth, waiting, expectant.

"But, why —?" I could see all his dreams shatter into dust. Myself, I was already imagining that warm stream.

"No buts — go ahead, pee on me." I wanted so much to sink into the ground, it was to be my pre-burial.

"No," he said. "No." He pulled up his underpants and his pants, and he went toward the door. "Dr. Moulton —" he said, when he turned at the door. "How could you ...?" words escaped him, and he was gone. I knew I would never see him again.

So, I have the letter now. I am reading and re-reading it. I can't quite believe it, but it's true. And I will, I promise you I will. I, Gloria Grahame, can do anything. I am somewhat magical in that way. I simply will not be discouraged by those who would say things about me. Let them talk. I think it will get out; the news will get out. The press is voracious, and they will have their way with me.

They will rape me. If I do this, I will be asking to be raped by the press, there is no denying that. But I, Gloria Grahame, will still act, because I can. It will be existential. I read a whole book about Jean-Paul Sartre once. I'm no dummy, you know. I'm not a rudderless ship. It's just that my rudder, unlike the rudders of other women, doesn't have some man holding on to it. It's my ship and I'll go where I want to, thank you. And when it comes down to it, if you don't like me that's the reason. You can claim that you disapprove of me; but you don't. You are merely jealous and wish you could be like me. What really makes you angry is the fact that I do whatever the hell I want, and that's something you just can't do. Well, I recommend that you try doing what I do, and running your own ship, instead of just being angry at me.

I, Gloria Grahame, am going to marry him. Yes, I'm going to marry Tony Ray. Yes, he's the son of Nicholas Ray, my ex-husband. Yes, it's something that people just don't do. But I'm going to do it. I, Gloria Grahame, don't give a fuck — and I really don't know why I have hesitated to swear in the past. I'm definitely not your kind of lady, the type of lady everyone wants me to be, so why the hell not?

He asked me. He asked me in his last letter. He's not old enough yet, so I'm going to wait. Yes, I'm capable of waiting. It's not just that I want to get into his pants, though I certainly want to do that. It's not about lust, although that is certainly a part of it. And speaking of parting, I simply can't part with him. We have shared too much.

And if you do not understand, then go right ahead. Don't understand. It's up to you. But don't think you can trample on me. Do you know the image on the old American

Revolutionary flag? During the war with Britain, before this became America? It's a drawing of a snake, coiled, ready to strike, and the motto reads: "Don't tread on me." Do not think I will ever be below you, or that I play by your rules. You have a right to dismiss me, or take the piss, or even to take a piss on me. But you will not find me on the ground. I am, and always will be, standing. Erect.

Make of that what you will.

That is all I wrote of Gloria. When I began to write about her marriage with Tony nothing would come out. It was very disconcerting.

I can't help relating a story about my first lover, who was eighteen years old; it is only tangentially relevant, in the sense that he too was sad because he was unable to "finish." I relate to the story because I think it need only be a comic, not a tragic, ending.

I was only twenty-nine, but ever the old man with the carefree young. I thought myself thin and ugly; looking back on the photos of us it seems to me that I was quite ephemerally gorgeous and that he wasn't that attractive at all. At any rate, he was everything to me back then, because I was discovering another male body for the first time. He was my Adonis, and I was the ancient virago Venus — perhaps that's where the myth gained its potency for me — and I would pierce him in the thigh, nightly, with a virulent ferocity; only it was not his thigh and I was not a boar. I suppose that made me a man, for a while. (But I didn't stay that way. He was the only man I ever did that to, and he was a boy at the time.) At any rate, he had another lover, which of course tortured me, and the other lover was closer to his age and a worthless dumb twit, but that didn't stop the torture, it only made it worse.

So one day, after I had done what I had to do (why do I feel reticent about using the usual expletive for human copulation — perhaps because I'm ashamed that I have *ever* played the active partner in sex, it just seems so "un-me"!) my beautiful boy was masturbating and trying to bring himself to orgasm and then he looked down at his lovely equipment, which was lying forlornly on his thigh, fat but limp. "There's nothing left." I asked him what he meant.

"Well, I was trying to come, but I had sex with Ricky today" (Oh, yes, the odious other: Ricky) "and then I pleasured myself" (There I go again. Why do I feel drawn to a less graphic terminology? Those are not the words he would have used, but, anyway …) "but there was nothing left," he said. "I don't have any left." It was difficult to feel sorry for him for having used up his bodily fluids in such a selfish, hedonistic way. But it was also oddly touching.

And that is the way I felt trying to write Gloria after her marriage to Tony. I see it as touching and faintly humorous now; back then it was frightening. There is nothing left. The only thing that had redeemed me was that I was always Gloria, on paper — how can I *be* her if I don't *write* her? But try as I might she wouldn't come out. It was my worst nightmare.

And then I thought about her later life. She had married Tony, and they lived together happily for so many years, and had children. This was contentment. And I couldn't believe it myself that she had ended up "happily." (True, she eventually broke up with Tony, but only after fourteen years of marriage.)

Hollywood recently made a movie about Gloria Grahame as an old woman — actually, with Annette Bening playing her — *Film Stars Don't Die in Liverpool*. I watched, and it somewhat ruined her later life for me. Don't misunderstand me, Annette Bening was gorgeous in it — a kind of reincarnation of Gloria Grahame — but there was only the slightest mention of the most tragic and compelling act of her life, that is the seduction of the young Tony, her stepson (there was only a mention of this by her nasty sister). So this primal incident in her life was somewhat glossed over in the film. This was so discouraging. This was not my Glorious Gloria, who had defied convention in no uncertain terms. For what had drawn me to her, to being her, was that we both were equally horrified by contentment.

I have been dedicated to sabotaging my life and could never be happy, period. Thus I was terribly attracted to her perverse affection for Nicholas Ray — their love so doomed from the beginning — and applauded her proud persistence in not only putting up with his violence, but to some degree enjoying it. And then the final taboo, the one that leads to death and destruction in Greek tragedy (but instead Gloria's Phaedra was triumphant) — seducing her own stepson! And with a certain élan; not only escaping tragedy but triumphing over that ogre of a husband.

But then comes the marriage to Tony and the kids and, well, literally, what can I say? A "happily ever after" just doesn't sit well with me, if for no other reason than I simply have no idea how to write her under those alarmingly un-perilous circumstances. "Tony's equipment is more than adequate — unlike his father's — and he loves me in sensitive ways I never imagined"? No, no, never. Suddenly, her life has become a corny rom-com and I have lost interest.

All this, perhaps, will explain my attitude to my own life; which may have confused you. I must tell you that when I was eating at Pratfalls the other evening — all alone, of course — a very contemporary pair of homosexuals entered. They were definitely "gay," in every sense of the word — one was somewhat older than the other, and one was slightly more effeminate, if you took a close look; but they were obviously also a normal — possibly married — couple. Both of them would have considered themselves "masculine" I am sure (even if inside they are not). They were soon joined by an attractive young trendy heterosexual couple. They seemed to be having a marvellous time. That is, until at one point I had a bit of an argument with the waiter (the first time, it seems to me, Pratfalls hired an arrogant young man to wait on tables). I, unfortunately, raised my voice to scold him, and it took on a prissy and petulant tone, which is certainly unbecoming and undeniably feminine. When my voice reached a certain pitch, the table of "normal" people — both straight and gay — stopped their conversation and stared at me. I immediately lowered my voice and tried to apologize to the waiter. I notice the married gay couple were evidently embarrassed by me. They looked at each other conspiratorially and then whispered their obvious disapproval to their trendy heterosexual friends. They were, it was clear, laughing at me. You see, I do not fit, even among those who might be considered to be my "own kind."

Indeed, all around me are happy, married homosexuals, many of them who seem like "normal" people. They do not engage in or even desire the kind of nightly activities or "perversions" I engage in, and many are impossible to differentiate from straight men. These men are not my friends. They are not my lovers. Why? Partially because many of them also reject me. They reject me because I represent to them a persistent reminder of their own effeminacy, or their own attraction to effeminate men. But I reject them, too. I do not want their happy lives, living in a culture that I know doesn't value who they are or what they like to do. In this way I am a rebel; though some might find my rebellion self-defeating. I was originally attracted to Pierre's leather jacket — I wondered what a leather jacket might symbolize in the present age. At one time it meant rebellion — and more than that a homosexual fantasy world of over-the-top butch men and girly femmes. It was another culture, one that seemed somehow at one time to make a place for men like me. Now there is no place for me, or who I am, and I am not one who wishes to lie to myself or other people, even in the smallest way, or can stand to see anyone else lie about themselves. I'm happy that Gloria found her Tony — but there is a part of me that also sees that as a compromise; that she has settled and is no longer the Gloria I once knew. The fact that I won't settle; is that perhaps my Achilles heel?

What am I to do? Where am I to go? I now know that my place is lower than the ground and my fate is to religiously roll in the dirt while a beautiful young man sends a golden stream of magical bitter-tasting boy liquid into my mouth, a liquid that cascades sadly — but sparkling still in the lamplight — over my aged, worthless, wrinkled, impotent body. This is now all I long for. But if I must sin, I need my redemption. I need my Gloria. Oh, Gloria, where hast thou gone?

Existing without her is terrible for me. But I have incorporated her. Or, more appropriately, I have realized that, however the world may see me, inside I am Venus. Or, more specifically, I am Lana Turner *playing* Venus (the high priestess "Astarte") in *The Prodigal*.

You must google it.

No — go directly to Google Images. Now!

Lana insisted on designing her own costumes for Astarte, and indeed they are beyond the pale. Most of them are simply sequins pasted together not-so-discreetly — which do little to disguise her nether regions. Two giant sequinned breastplates barely cover her resplendent breasts. The costumes she crafted for that movie are beyond camp. In one publicity photo she rises majestically from a pink half-shell, every inch Shakespeare's Hollywood Goddess, relentlessly predatory, her arms extended in a rather menacing way, sporting a come-hither look that seems to desperately demand erect obedience.

Outside, of course, I am still Denton. But because I have Venus inside, because I have incorporated — and drowned myself in — a kind of triumphant otherness, one that has a sexual and even (perhaps from far away) a loving component, I don't know if I need to write Gloria anymore. I thought I was dooming myself to both a corporeal and sexual death, when, in fact, I have blossomed into a transgressive, gloriously bent being.

Certainly, I still exist in reality. (Whatever that is?) But I have given up all hope of ever directing a stage version of *Venus and Adonis*. And I will go nowhere near poor Pierre — who I had forced into sentient adulthood when I made him my "modest proposal." I am still invisible to most people, although I am still occasionally accosted by monsters who are horrified by my mannerisms and say awful things to me. But now — inside — I know that I am Venus, a secret, gorgeous, sacrilegious catastrophe beyond measure, and nothing else matters.

Because, as for — well, you know. *That?* Yes, yes, you will find me, more often than not, on weekends, in a dark corner somewhere in a sauna or a bathroom or a dark room, or an alley even (when the weather is temperate), wet from a golden shower administered by a beautiful young man. This is my fate, and I embrace it. There is, after all, an exaltation in that. If you haven't embraced the freedom and licence of abjection you should give it a try. It really, really is quite a lot of fun. A miserable existence you say? Oh, no, I dare to disagree.

I am about to step out the door now. How sweet it is to say goodbye! For the writerly Denton was only facilitating Gloria, and now she — or rather Venus — is inside.

I'm off to the races, or — you know where … Any dark place where young men wander and have needs. I won't go into gross detail.

I'm turning up the collar of my rather frayed coat, as it's an oddly cool fall evening. (I daren't part with that coat because it is *beyond* style.) I'm turning off the lights in my little room where I wrote it all. I'm peering out the back window. It's a window that no one sees. That's what I like best and where I belong. I see everything.

But no one sees me.

Acknowledgements

I want to acknowledge Russell Smith's extraordinary help and support. At last, thanks!

Sky Gilbert is a writer, director, professor, and drag queen extraordinaire. For more than forty years, he has been one of the most controversial forces on the Canadian arts scene. He was co-founder and artistic director of Toronto's Buddies in Bad Times Theatre — one of the world's largest gay and lesbian theatres — from 1979 to 1997. He has had more than forty plays produced and has won three Dora Mavor Moore Awards for *The Whore's Revenge*, *Suzie Goo, Private Secretary*, and *The Situationists*. He has written seven critically acclaimed novels and three award-winning poetry collections. He won the 2005 ReLit award for his novel *An English Gentleman*, and his collection of "anti-essays," *Small Things*, won the Hamilton Literary Award for non-fiction in 2019. Sky has written a number of articles for the online free speech journal Quillette as well as for his inappropriately titled blog, *Another Blog That Nobody Reads*. He is a professor of creative writing and theatre at the University of Guelph. An ex-American who has lived most of his life in Canada, Sky now resides in Hamilton, Ontario, with a cat named Jizzy.